CHOCK FULL OF CHRISTMAS

A HEARTSPRINGS VALLEY WINTER TALE (BOOK 5)

ANNE CHASE

THOMAS PUBLISHING

ISBN-13: 978-1-945320-06-4

In memory of Rena and Elizabeth

CHAPTER 1

$\mathcal{T}$he most important Christmas season of Abby Donovan's life began on a crisp, sunny afternoon in late November inside her warm and cozy chocolate shop overlooking Heartsprings Valley's town square.

She stood behind her counter, brushing a lock of brown hair from her cheek, as she watched her latest gaggle of customers scoot out of the store. The customers — tourists from Boston, up north visiting relatives for Thanksgiving — had been a cheerful bunch, eagerly loading up on boxes of Abby's hand-made chocolates to enjoy during their long drive home, their enthusiasm and laughter filling the tiny store and bringing a smile to Abby's lips.

A glance at the display counter confirmed that the Boston gaggle had cleaned her out of salted caramels, one of her most popular chocolates. From instinct born of long practice, she grabbed her planning sheet and wrote, "S.C. — 4 dozen." If the store got quiet later, she might have time to make more before closing. If not, well, that meant yet another early start tomorrow morning.

Just like every morning, she thought, the smile fading away. Setting the pen down, she allowed herself to settle onto the stool behind the counter and stretch her back. She'd been going all day; the moment of quiet and rest was welcome. Idly, she plucked at her sweater, a red-and-green holiday-themed number that was appropriately festive but perhaps too warm for a long day in the shop. Over the shop's speakers, the town's radio station was playing a holiday favorite.

Yes, she thought as she hummed along, it was beginning to look a lot like Christmas. Outside, an early snow already dusted the ground, with more forecast to arrive that evening. Squinting against the afternoon sun streaming through the storefront window, she gazed across the street into the center of the town square, where a group of volunteers were stringing Christmas lights along the edge of the town's clamshell bandstand. The little New England town she now called home had, like most places, its own special rhythms, as sure and reliable as the changing seasons. After eight years here, she knew them well. Soon enough — tomorrow, if the snow came as promised — folks would be busy building the snowpeople and snow-animals that Heartsprings Valley was famous for.

Eight years. The thought brought her up short. *How the time had flown.* It seemed just yesterday that she'd moved up here and opened Abby's Chocolate Heaven. Her eyes roamed the walls of her shop, checking again to make sure her holiday decorations — the garlands of holly, ornaments galore, and ribbons of red and green that she took out of storage every year — were hung with care.

Her eyes landed on her laptop in front of her on the counter. Inside that little machine was a seemingly endless list of necessary chores. The day had been frenetic — the Saturday after Thanksgiving was always among the busiest days of the year — and she was behind on so many of her usual tasks.

With a sigh, she grabbed the laptop and was about to start adding expenses into the budget spreadsheet when she heard the shop bell sound. The door opened and a stranger stepped in. He stood at the door for a moment, a smile lighting up his handsome face as he breathed in the shop's welcoming aroma of cocoa and spices. Carefully, he shut the door behind him, his gaze roving over the decorations covering every inch of the walls.

He didn't see her at first. When his eyes found hers behind the counter, he blinked.

"Hi," he said, his voice clear but hesitant.

"Good afternoon. Is there something I can help you with?"

As the stranger approached, she found herself absorbing details about him. He was a tall man, about her age — mid-forties — with an athletic build and an open, friendly face, dressed in jeans and boots and mackinaw. His full head of short-cropped brown hair showed flecks of grey. His brown eyes peered at her uncertainly.

"You have a great place," he said. "It smells amazing in here. What's the scent? Cocoa, with a hint of … cinnamon?"

"That's right. Good nose."

He bent down to check out the display counter with its rows of tempting chocolates — the gorgeous truffles, nougats, caramels, brittles, and more that Abby took such pride in.

"The selection is incredible. I hear you make all of them?"

"Each and every one."

He stood up and extended his hand. "I should introduce myself. John Buckley."

"Abby Donovan." The instant her hand slipped into his, she felt it: a tremor, an undercurrent — a spark.

John's eyes widened. For a long second, he stared at her, as if surprised. His hand felt so strong and warm.

"My daughter and son are with my parents

— they'll be here in a minute," he said, withdrawing his hand, seemingly with reluctance. "Before they arrive, there's something I'd like to ask."

Abby's eyebrows rose. "Ask away." A rush of unwanted questions came from nowhere, unbidden and completely irrelevant to the situation: Why no ring on the third finger of his left hand? Why mention his kids but not his wife? Was he divorced, perhaps?

Other thoughts crowded in as well. How did her hair look? What about her face? When this stranger — John, he'd said — gazed at her, what was he seeing? Usually she felt comfortable with her appearance — her figure on the slim side, her face nice enough, her shoulder-length brown hair actually capable of looking pretty good, at least on occasion — but the shop was warm and the sweater heavy and maybe she was coming across as sweaty or flushed or disheveled?

Urgh. She was being so silly!

John stayed silent for a second, as if also gripped by an uncertainty of his own, then said, "I hear you offer chocolate-making classes."

"I do," she said, relieved to hear a safe topic.

"I have your flyer," he said, pulling a copy from his jacket pocket. "I was just over in the bookstore and Maggie — my daughter — asked if we could sign up for a class."

"We have a class in two weeks." Yes, chocolate

classes were definitely a no-stress subject. "Three hours on a Saturday afternoon."

"That'd be perfect. I'd like to sign up me and my daughter and my son."

"Great," she said, reaching under the counter for a clipboard with the signup sheet.

"Also," John said, glancing toward the door, "I wanted to ask about something else."

"Sure." She handed him the signup sheet and a pen. This John fellow certainly was being mysterious. Which she found … intriguing.

"I guess you could call it a surprise Christmas present of sorts," he said as he wrote down the signup information. He was about to say more when the shop door burst open and a boisterous quartet barreled in. Two kids — a boy and a girl, both about ten — led the charge, followed by a man and woman in their seventies.

John turned, startled. "Hey," he said to them. "You're here."

"Dad," the girl said with a thrilled gasp, her eyes widening as she took in the shop's decorations. "This place is *awesome*."

The boy zoomed right to the counter and pointed. "*Whoa.* That's the one I want."

The girl turned to her brother. "How do you know? You don't even know what it is."

"I don't need to," the boy said. "It's the biggest one."

Abby smiled. The kids were adorable — bundled up for winter with matching red scarfs, rosy cheeks, and light brown hair. The thought came: Were they twins?

John cleared his throat. "Kids, introduce yourselves to Ms. Donovan."

The girl turned her gaze to Abby and extended her hand. "Ms. Donovan? Hi, I'm Maggie."

Abby returned the shake. "Very pleased to meet you, Maggie. Please, call me Abby."

"Is this your chocolate shop?"

"Indeed it is."

"I love this place so much," the girl said, very emphatically. "It's perfect. It's like a dream come to life."

Abby laughed. "I'm glad to hear that." She turned to the boy and extended her hand. "I'm Abby. Welcome to my shop."

The boy accepted her handshake. "I'm Jacob." He pointed to the chocolate he'd been eyeing. "What's that one?"

"I call that the Crunchy Marshmallow Cherry Supreme. It's a marshmallow caramel swirl with a candied cherry center, dipped in milk chocolate, and sprinkled with crisped rice."

"Is it the biggest one?"

"It is. It also has a nice big taste."

"Dad, you said we could pick whichever one we wanted, right?"

John turned to Abby. "We all just had lunch and a dessert, but in a moment of weakness, I agreed they could each get one piece of chocolate as an afternoon treat."

"Well, you came to the right place," Abby said.

"I'd like to introduce my parents, Betsy and Don."

As Abby shifted her attention to them, she realized that John's mom seemed familiar. "Betsy, have we met before?"

"Briefly, a few weeks back," Betsy said. "I popped in with a friend." She was a short woman with a short gray bob and a bright, bubbly manner. "We live over in Eagle Cove — Don and I, that is — but I've been hearing about your shop for ages and finally had a chance to swing by. Everyone keeps raving about Abby's Chocolate Heaven."

"Welcome back," Abby said, then gestured to the kids. "Out for a day with the grandkids?"

"Oh, yes. Every chance we get."

"What have you all been up to today?"

"First thing was cleanup at John's house — we stayed over for Thanksgiving rather than drive back and forth to Eagle Cove — and let me tell you, the kitchen needed a good scrubbing after all the holiday hoo-haw, though yesterday we were too stuffed full of turkey and pie and stuffing — ha! — to be any good to anyone. So this morning we got everything back in order." She paused for breath, then rushed on. "Then we decided to get out of the house and move our legs, so we walked here — John and the kids live nearby, about ten minutes away, which makes for a nice stroll when the sun is out like it is today — and went to the bookstore and a couple of other shops — this little town square of yours is so charming! — and now we're here."

"Grandma," Maggie said, tugging at Betsy's coat sleeve, "which chocolate should I get?"

"Oh, my," Betsy said, stepping closer to peer at the rows of chocolates filling the displays. "That's a tough one. There are so many delicious-looking choices."

Jacob said, "I know which one I'm getting."

Maggie pressed her forehead against the counter window, peering with concentration. Abby glanced at John and found him smiling at his daughter.

Abby cleared her throat. "Maybe I can help?"

Maggie gazed up at her uncertainly. "Sure?"

"What are some of your preferences?"

The girl considered the question. "What do you mean?"

"Do you prefer milk chocolate? Dark chocolate?"

"Milk chocolate," she said right away.

"Nuts or no nuts?"

"Maybe … no nuts?"

"Smooth and silky, or something with a nice crunch?"

Maggie's brow furrowed. "Maybe … a crunch?"

"Okay, we're getting close. Final question: Marsh-mallow, caramel, or cherry filling?"

The girl's eyes widened. How to decide? After a second, she said, "Can I have all of them?"

"Sure," Abby said. "But that will mean picking the same chocolate as your brother."

Jacob shot his sister a triumphant look. "See? Told you it's the right one."

Maggie glared at him, clearly bothered that her preference matched his.

"It's perfectly okay for you to like the same thing," Abby said. "It's also perfectly okay for your decision-making to follow different paths."

"My path is better," Maggie said. "At least I know what I'm picking before I pick it."

"All you do is waste time," Jacob retorted. "My path is better because it's quicker."

"Kids," John said, stepping in, "remember what we talked about." To Abby, he said apologetically, "Sometimes, the twins need to be reminded that differences can be a source of strength and are deserving of respect, especially when working together."

"So you're twins," Abby said, pleased that her hunch was right.

"Ten years old and growing up way too fast," John said.

"I was born first," Jacob said. "I'm the oldest."

"By two whole minutes — big deal," Maggie shot back immediately.

Abby hid a smile. She suspected the twins' birth order would be a lifelong source of friendly sibling rivalry.

John said, "Okay, kids, time to decide what you want. We'll take the chocolate to the lake from here."

"We're going on a hike," Jacob told Abby. "Up on the ridge."

"Oh, it's beautiful up there," Abby said. "The views of the town and the lake are spectacular."

Betsy stepped closer and asked anxiously, "How steep is it? Will we be able to keep up?"

"If you can walk around town, you can walk the ridge trail," Abby said. "The trail rises gently, at least for the most part."

"We'll be fine," Don said, speaking up for the first time. "And if not, we'll head back down." He was a trim man with kind eyes and a full head of white hair. As he spoke, Abby realized how much he and John resembled each other, with the same lean build, handsome features, and patient demeanor.

John said, "Kids, you settled on your picks?"

"I have," Jacob said.

Maggie's mouth tightened, her eyes stuck on the tempting Crunchy Marshmallow Cherry Supreme. "Yes," she finally said.

"Should I bag them up?" Abby asked John.

"That'd be great."

"Anything for the grownups?"

Betsy said, "Don and I will pop in tomorrow before we head home. I can't wait to get a box of your chocolates to share with the folks back in Eagle Cove."

"Sounds great."

John was bending lower again, examining the options carefully. "I'll take a dark chocolate with the coffee ganache."

Inwardly, Abby applauded his choice. The piece he'd selected was one of her favorites — not as sweet as the others, with a sharpness that some interpreted as bitterness but which she appreciated for its complexity and depth.

"Dad," Maggie said. "Did you remember to —"

"Sign us up for a chocolate-making class?" John said. "I sure did. Abby has a class for us in two weeks."

Maggie whirled toward Abby. "For real?"

Abby laughed — the girl's enthusiasm was infectious. "Yes, Maggie, for real."

"What are we going to make?"

Abby reached under the counter and pulled out a brochure. "Here's a description of the chocolates. Read through this and we can decide during class."

Maggie accepted the brochure as if receiving a treasure. "Thank you."

"Kids," John said, "what do you say to Abby?"

"Thank you, Abby," the twins said in unison.

"Great meeting you both," Abby said. "Look forward to seeing you in two weeks."

"Me, too!" Maggie said, her excitement obvious.

As John hustled everyone out the door, he turned to Abby, raised his hand to his cheek like he was talking into a phone, and mouthed, "I'll call you."

Then he and his family were gone, leaving Abby with an unanswered question.

No, more than that — a mystery.

Before his family arrived, John had been about to ask her a question. But he hadn't asked it. So what was his question?

Clearly, it had something to do with the "Christmas surprise" he mentioned.

But what role did he envision Abby playing in it?

CHAPTER 2

*T*he solution to the mystery came half an hour later, when the store's phone rang, Abby picked up and heard a voice say, "Hi, Ms. Donovan? It's John Buckley."

"Good afternoon, John. And please, call me Abby."

"Sure, Abby." In the background, she heard what sounded like a gust of wind. "Sorry about the noise. We just started up the trail and it's a bit windy."

"The weather can be unpredictable up there — take care. But don't worry, I can hear you fine."

John lowered his voice. "The kids are up ahead, so I figured I should call and ask while I can."

Here it was: the Christmas surprise he'd brought up earlier. "Ask away."

"I don't know how else to say it, so I'll just come

out with it. If possible, I'd like to sign up for private classes to learn how to make chocolates."

Abby paused. The request was *not* what she was expecting. "I think we can probably arrange that...."

"I'm hoping we can do the private classes *before* the class with the kids."

Abby's eyebrows rose. "Can I ask why?"

"It's for my daughter. I want the two of us to have something — an activity, a hobby — that we can do together. Jacob and I have hockey — I'm a coach for his team. But Maggie loves baking and cooking — that's what she's really passionate about. And the unfortunate thing is...."

A smile crept to Abby's lips. She already knew what the next words out his mouth would be.

"I'm a disaster in the kitchen."

Bingo. Abby resisted the urge to chuckle. "So you're thinking...."

"I'm thinking, maybe I could get a head start on the chocolate-making and not be completely hopeless at it — with your help, of course. That way, she and I could start doing stuff together in the kitchen that might actually end up being, you know, *edible*."

His request was clear and his voice was confident, but Abby sensed an undercurrent of anxiety in his tone. *He really wants this*, she thought.

Her eyes darted to her calendar. Did she have time? The class with the kids was in two weeks. Was there a way to squeeze in private lessons between now and then?

"John," she said, "I'd be happy to help you. Maggie is adorable. But the question is when…."

"About that, I have a suggestion. On Wednesday nights, Grandma and Grandpa usually drive over for dinner and spend the night, and I usually use that evening to catch up on work and other stuff. If that time works for you, perhaps we could do classes the next two Wednesday evenings?"

Abby swallowed. With a specific day and time now on the table, she had a decision to make: Did she want to do this? She didn't need to consult her calendar to know that on Wednesday evenings, she was nearly always in the shop, either up front helping customers or in the back making more chocolates in the kitchen.

"How about this," she said. "For the next few weeks, I'll be keeping the shop open later for holiday shoppers. If you're okay with me occasionally needing to go up front to help customers, we can do private lessons in the shop's kitchen for the next two Wednesdays, from seven to nine. How does that sound?"

"That sounds perfect," John said, his voice full of relief and enthusiasm. Abby realized she liked how his voice sounded when he was pleased. "So I'll see you on Wednesday?"

"Wednesday at seven. Enjoy your hike."

"Thank you, Abby. I really appreciate this."

And he was gone.

Abby stared at the phone for a second, then set it down. Why had she just agreed to private lessons with a stranger during her busiest season of the year? Was it the adorable kids? The enthusiasm in Maggie's eyes? The mixture of desperation and hope in John's voice?

She sighed, vexed with herself. Really, she needed to think through her decisions better.

As the thought rolled through her head, she went still and frowned. Something she'd just said had resonated. For a while now, she'd been conscious of a feeling, an awareness, creeping up on her. And for reasons she couldn't even begin to fathom, John's request — and her agreement to help him — had finally crystallized that awareness into a feeling — no, more than that, a *truth* — that apparently she'd been avoiding:

Her small shop was bursting at the seams.

And she was running out of steam.

She breathed in sharply as the realization swept through her, the impact sharp and almost painful. After eight years of pouring her heart and soul and every waking moment into running the chocolate shop of her dreams, she could feel her energy and commitment fading. The reality had been sneaking up on her for months but she hadn't wanted to deal with it.

Slowly and surely, she was losing her passion. It was a frightening feeling.

She cast her eyes over her little shop, tears threatening. She loved this place. She loved being a chocolatier. She had no regrets — not a one — about the leap she'd taken eight years ago.

But was this dream, this small business she'd built from scratch, enough for her now?

No, she heard herself say. *Not even close.*

Angrily, she brushed back a tear. Now was not the time for painful self-examination. She had things to do this afternoon. A shop to run. She could poke and prod and pry at this unsettling revelation later.

That's when she heard it — the door opening.

Saved by the bell, she thought gratefully, turning away to give her eyes a quick wipe.

Behind her, she heard a familiar and very lovely voice say:

"Yoooo-hoo, guess who!"

CHAPTER 3

*A*bby grinned as she finished dabbing her eyes. She knew all too well that this particular yoo-hooer loved making an entrance — even when the stage was a tiny chocolate store and she had an audience of just one.

"Melody!" Abby said, turning around with a laugh and hustling from behind the counter to give her friend a hug. "You're back!"

"Finally, yes, I'm back," Melody said, returning the hug with warmth. "A month away from Heartsprings Valley is a month too long. It's so good to see you and to breathe in the lovely, welcoming air of this wonderful store."

Abby pulled back to take in her friend. Part of her still couldn't believe that she, Abby Donovan, was actually friends with Melody Connelly, the famous Broadway star. For a split second, Abby flashed to the memory of their first meeting, three years ago in this very spot, on a winter afternoon much like this one. The shop door had burst open and a whirlwind of energy — a tall, beautiful woman with lovely green eyes and a rich tumble of red hair — had strode in. As striking as the woman was, what had truly set her apart was her enthusiasm. Her confidence and high spirits were breathtaking — they seemed to flow from her effortlessly.

On that day, after pronouncing the shop "adorable," Melody had asked if Abby was open to filming a chocolate-making segment for Melody's social media. Overwhelmed, Abby hadn't known what to say at first. But quickly enough, she'd recognized the benefits and managed to say yes.

The decision, it turned out, had been a good one. The video session in her tiny kitchen had ended up being really fun. Abby had never done anything on camera — she'd been a bundle of nerves — but Melody had sensed Abby's anxiety and quickly put her at ease. Over the course of the afternoon, her famous guest had revealed herself to be a good listener and an attentive student. Beneath that glamorous exterior beat a kind heart. The segment, when it aired, had done a wonderful job of showcasing Abby's Chocolate Heaven.

And the orders that came flying in — goodness! For several weeks after the video was posted, it was all Abby could do to keep up. Even now, three years later, she received inquiries and orders from complete strangers who'd just watched the video and simply had to try a box of Abby's handmade chocolates.

A lot had changed for her famous friend in the past three years. Charmed by Heartsprings Valley, Melody had bought a crumbling old manse on the ridge outside of town, restored it to its original glory, and met and fallen in love with James, a local furniture craftsman. Their wedding, just three months earlier, had been a lovely affair on the lawn of the big house on the hill, full of joy and dancing and laughter.

"When did you get back?" Abby asked. She'd hadn't seen her friend in over a month — Melody had spent much of the autumn in L.A. filming a movie. But she still had that newlywed glow.

"Late last night," Melody said, breathing in deeply. "Oh, I wish I could bottle up this shop and take it with me wherever I go."

Abby laughed. "Wouldn't *that* be something."

"*Chocolate Heaven by Abby* — that's what we'll call it." Melody gave her a teasing smile. "I'll help with the branding and promotion."

"What brings you here today?"

"Oh, a million things. I was just over at the hardware store. That big old gorgeous house of mine needs constant attention — there's always something with that place — but I couldn't resist swinging by to see you. I want to invite you to an impromptu get-together, two weeks from tomorrow."

"Sounds fun. What's the occasion?"

"I'm planning a surprise for James."

Melody's eyes were twinkling with excitement. Clearly, she was very pleased with herself.

"A surprise?" Abby said. "What's the occasion?"

"To celebrate the opening of his new furniture workshop."

"The workshop is finished? That's wonderful."

"The architect called and said the final steps are ahead of schedule — they're on track to wrap up this week."

"Just in time for Christmas."

"James has been very involved in the construction, of course, but last week I dragged him out to L.A. for the final week of the shoot, and he doesn't know the workshop is ahead of schedule. So I thought, why not do something to celebrate? And the best part: He has no idea!"

Abby restrained the urge to laugh. "You two are made for each other."

"I'm a very lucky woman and I know it."

Abby swallowed back a surge of emotion. Melody and James were, in fact, an amazing couple. "Speaking of James, where is he?"

"Still in L.A. meeting with new clients — checking out their homes, getting measurements, finalizing plans for custom furniture."

"And then he's heading home?"

Melody sighed. "Well, that was the idea. The entire time I was in L.A., I was dreaming about Christmas here. The plan was for us to be in Heartsprings Valley the entire holiday season and get everything ready for our big gathering — my mom's coming up, along with friends from New York. But I got a call last night, literally the moment I got home. The director needs reshoots — so I have to fly back to L.A. tonight."

"Oh, that's too bad. How long will you be gone?"

She sighed again. "Two weeks. But not a day longer — the director promised."

"So you'll still be here in plenty of time for Christmas."

"Yes, but it means that, for the second year in a row, I'll be scrambling to get everything done in time."

Abby gave her friend's hand a squeeze. "You need anything, just ask."

"Thank you. But I wouldn't dream of imposing — I know how busy you are this time of year. Fortunately, the architect for the workshop has volunteered to help get everything ready for the surprise party."

"Oh, that's great."

"Though you know, there is one thing," Melody said, her eyes drawn to the counter display and the tempting rows of chocolates. "Any chance you can squeeze in an order of chocolates for the party?"

"Of course."

Melody glanced at the wall shelves loaded with freshly packed boxes of chocolates awaiting purchase. "Also, I'd love to take some of these with me back to L.A. — the film crew will adore them."

"How many?" Abby asked.

"As many as you can spare. Maybe a half-dozen boxes?"

The two of them got busy packing up the boxes and getting Melody's party order settled.

"So," Melody said, switching gears, "how are things with you?"

"Busy as always."

"Anything new to report?"

Sadly, not a single thing, she almost admitted. "Just trying to stay on top of stuff."

"You know," Melody said, her gaze becoming thoughtful, "we're going to have to do something about you."

"What do you mean?" Abby said, instantly on alert.

"We need to get you a honey."

Oh, geez. Melody had said this before, but Abby now sensed a newfound seriousness. "Melody, no. I'm fine."

Her friend was nodding to herself, clearly

warming to the idea. "Yes, I'm going to set you up with someone."

"No, you're not."

"Yes, I am."

"Melody!"

"Darling, think of it as a grand adventure."

Abby sighed. "Clearly, you've been infected by the world-famous Heartsprings Valley meddling bug."

Melody laughed. "Yes, indeed. Bite marks all over. I've got it bad."

"Please, Melody...."

"You'll thank me, I promise. I'm a born match-maker. My track record is excellent." She then rattled off a list of names of people Abby didn't know — friends of hers from New York, presumably — who were now happily coupled.

From long experience, Abby knew there was no winning this argument — meddlers loved nothing more than bragging about their clever and inspired schemes — so she tried to change the subject. "Tell me more about the surprise you're planning for James."

"We'll throw the party in the workshop," Melody said, taking the bait. "Late afternoon. James won't know a thing about it, of course. I'll come up with some reason for us to be away from the house that afternoon."

"Where will everyone park?" Abby asked,

mindful that the workshop and Abby's manse were in a wooded lot at the top of the ridge — which meant parked cars in the long driveway and open area out front would be a clear giveaway.

Melody's brow furrowed. "Good point."

"You could probably use the school bus," Abby suggested.

"The school bus?"

"It's a big old-fashioned yellow school bus. Just call the principal. She rents it out all the time — the extra money helps pay for school supplies and activities. You can have your guests meet in the school parking lot, and the bus can shuttle everyone up."

Melody's grin widened as the idea took shape. "Darling, you are the best. What would I do without you? What would my life be like if I had never discovered Heartsprings Valley?"

"I can't answer that one," Abby said with a smile.

Melody's eyes flickered with amusement. "And for the record, I know what you just did."

"What did I just do?"

"The little trick you just pulled. Distracting me from my new goal of introducing you to the right fellow. Nice try, but it didn't work." She glanced at her watch. "However, I am granting you a reprieve. Normally I'd be peppering you with detailed questions about the man of your dreams. Alas, I have too many errands to complete this afternoon, and too little time to get them all done. So I must press the pause button on our manhunt and bid you adieu."

Melody reached out and clasped Abby's hands. "See you in two weeks?"

"Count on it."

CHAPTER 4

*S*everal hours later, after a long and busy afternoon behind the counter, Abby pulled on her winter coat, grabbed her handbag, and turned out the lights. She paused at the front door, her hand on the knob, and ran through her mental checklist to make sure she hadn't forgotten anything. Kitchen lights off — check. Back door locked — check. Heat turned down — check. Phone and wallet in handbag — check. Box of chocolates in handbag — check.

Satisfied, she made her way out and locked up for the night. Normally, her next move would be to head through the town square to begin her twelve-minute walk home, but tonight was her monthly Book Club gathering at her friend Elsie's, just a block away in the opposite direction. She found her gaze drawn to the shop's window display. In addition to the usual assortment of tempting chocolates, the display boasted something that was quickly becoming a Christmas tradition: an exquisitely designed gingerbread house made by her friend Becca, the town librarian. For this year's display, Becca had chosen to depict the bandstand in the middle of the town square, decorated with tiny Christmas lights and faithful in every way to the real thing. On the gingerbread stage, a chorus of snowpeople were singing their hearts out for an appreciative audience of even more snowpeople. Each tiny snowperson was exquisitely decorated with a hat, eyes, nose, mouth, and buttons. The effect was charming and humorous, and Abby marveled again at how Becca — with a library, a three-year-old, and a husband to take care of — managed to find the time.

Abby turned her thoughts to the evening ahead. She always enjoyed Book Club. In addition to some actual discussion of books, the gatherings were a chance to see her friends and catch up, which wasn't always easy to do with everyone so busy.

The soft crunch of snow underfoot carried through the still night air. She sensed a hint — a taste, really — of approaching snow. A blanket of fresh powder was exactly what Heartsprings Valley needed to kick off the Christmas season in true winter style. Soon enough, if the forecast held, Becca's vision of snowpeople filling the town square would be a happy reality.

She turned off the square onto a tree-lined residential street. The homes on the block, built on larger lots, dated back well over a century. Elsie's house was a two-story Victorian halfway down the street, painted cream with blue and gold trim, with a separate garage in the rear. Through the front windows, Abby glimpsed Christmas tree lights blinking merrily away. Elsie preferred her friends to enter through the mudroom off the kitchen, so Abby made her way up the long driveway to the back. While stamping her boots on the back porch to brush off clinging snow, she spied a light in the garage and heard the faint sound of Christmas songs coming from within, accompanied by the bang of metal on metal.

She smiled. From the sound of it, Elsie's husband Bert, the town's mayor, was tinkering away in the garage. Knowing him, he was probably making sure his trusty old snowplow was in good working order in preparation for whatever Mother Nature was about to throw their way.

Abby knocked twice on the back door, then stepped into the mudroom. "Elsie, it's Abby," she called out.

A familiar voice yelled from the kitchen, "Evening, dear!"

Abby shrugged out of her coat and scarf, hung them on a hook, and made her way into the kitchen, where Elsie was busy setting crackers and cheese on a plate. She paused her preparations to give Abby a hug. "How are you? When's the last time I saw you?"

"Last month, I think?"

"A month? Unbelievable. We're all too busy, aren't we? You're the first one here."

A kindly woman in her sixties with curly gray hair, Elsie was in her usual getup — blue jeans, sweater, and comfortable white sneakers. Today's sweater, a blue wool number, boasted a line drawing in white of reindeer pulling a sleigh.

"How can I help?" Abby asked.

"Most everything's on the table, but if you could check the silverware situation…."

"Got it. I brought chocolates, by the way." Abby pulled the box from her handbag and headed into the dining room, where she ran her eye over a table already loaded with food — a mixed salad, Elsie's cheesy potato casserole, sandwich fixings, and more — along with bottles of water and wine.

Abby set the chocolates next to a freshly baked apple pie — which smelled scrumptious — then counted the number of forks, knives, and spoons next to the stack of plates. "How many are coming tonight?"

"Just five. You, me, Gail, Hettie Mae, and Clara."

"What about Bert?"

"Oh, he'll be keeping himself busy in the garage."

"Getting the snowplow ready?"

"Oh, that old thing is fine. He spied an antique generator at the salvage yard and decided to fix it."

"I didn't know he knew how to fix generators."

"He doesn't!" Elsie said with a laugh. "But since when did that stop him?"

Abby returned to the kitchen. "You're good with the silverware. Let me take that tray for you."

"Thank you."

At that moment, they heard two knocks, followed by a pair of voices announcing their arrival. A few seconds later, Gail and Hettie Mae bustled in.

"I brought wine," Gail said.

"Cookies for me," Hettie Mae added.

"You shouldn't have," Elsie said.

"Too late now," Hettie Mae said, giving her friend a quick hug.

Gail glanced at Abby. "Hey, you."

"Hey." Gail was a trim woman in her fifties, with a short bob of gray hair and an observant manner. She was one of the town's two veterinarians and Abby's closest friend. Dressed in her normal dark slacks and collared shirt, she had clearly come straight from work.

"Gail," Elsie said, pulling her in for a hug. "How was your Thanksgiving?"

"Oh, very nice," Gail replied. "Becca and Nick invited Abby and me and several others over."

"I'm still feeling the after-effects — way too much turkey," Abby added.

Hettie Mae spoke up. "Elsie, what did you and Bert do for Turkey Day?"

"Drove over to his nephew's — a big gathering there." Elsie peered into the oven. "Made for a nice change. No cleanup here for once. We're having nibblies tonight. Nothing fancy. I figured we could all use a break from food overload."

A smile came to Abby's lips. *Fat chance of that,* she almost said, thinking about the table weighted down with treats.

The four women made their way into the dining room.

"Elsie, look at this spread," Hettie Mae said. "You shouldn't have." She was a tall woman with an upright posture and a clear gaze. Her dress — she generally favored dresses over pants except in the coldest weather — was long-sleeved grey-and-black wool enlivened with a holiday broach of a grinning, sparkling snowman. For thirty years Hettie Mae been the town's devoted librarian. After happily settling into retirement, she and her husband had taken up cruising and now spent several months a year devoting their considerable energies to exploring the world.

Abby realized her gaze was being irresistibly drawn to the apple pie. Her stomach rumbled. She loved apple pie — all things apple-related, actually — almost as much as she loved chocolate.

"Baked it this afternoon," Elsie said.

Abby laughed. "Am I that obvious?"

Elsie handed her a knife. "Yes, dear, you are."

Hettie Mae said, "Abby, I heard you had a visit today from Betsy."

It took Abby a second, but she connected the dots. "Oh, from Eagle Cove? Yes, she and her family swung by the shop. Such a nice woman. How do you know her?"

"We go way back," Hettie Mae said with a wave. "She's a good person to know. Works as a dispatcher for the sheriff over there. Keeps her finger on the pulse."

And no doubt shares what she finds out, Abby thought but didn't say.

"Her son is an architect," Hettie Mae continued. "Moved here with his kids from Boston about a year ago."

"I met them today," Abby said.

"The son is a nice man. Of course, it's very sad about his wife."

Abby went still. She'd noticed the lack of a ring on the third finger of John's left hand – and the lack of any mention of the kids' mom during their conversations in the shop and on the phone. But Abby's assumption had been that John and his wife were divorced.

"Sad?" Abby asked. "What do you mean?"

"Cancer," Hettie Mae said. "Three years ago."

"Oh, my." Abby's thoughts went immediately to little Maggie and Jacob. "I'm so sorry to hear that."

Hettie Mae nodded. "Afterwards, I guess for the first couple of years, John tried to keep everything going in Boston, but it all got to be too much, so a year ago he moved the kids up here to be closer to their grandparents."

"Betsy and Don seem to enjoy being grandparents."

"Oh, they love it. And what's nice for me is that I get to see Betsy more often — she's over here every week."

At that moment, they heard a voice calling Elsie's name from the mudroom. A few seconds later, Clara bustled in, her cheeks flushed pink from the cold night air, a grocery bag in her arms.

"Evening, everyone," she said cheerfully. "Sorry I'm late!"

"You're not late at all," Elsie said. "Let me get that."

"I'm good," Clara said, setting the bag down carefully on the floor. She straightened back up with a small groan. "There are chocolate chip cookies in there somewhere, but mostly it's just empty containers. I brought dinner to Luke and his crew. They're still at the bandstand."

"Still there?" Hettie Mae said. "Whatever for?"

"Something wonky with the electrical panel. He's

trying to get everything in place before the snow hits."

Hettie Mae nodded. Clara's husband Luke worked as a general contractor and was frequently roped into fixing and setting up stuff for town events.

Clara set her handbag on a chair, unwound her red wool scarf, and shrugged out of her winter coat. She was a tiny slip of a woman, just shy of thirty, with shoulder-length brown hair, a pretty face and an energetic manner, who came across — quite accurately — as a mixture of friendly, organized, and forthright. Tonight she was wearing a bulky dark-blue sweater with her usual jeans and leather boots.

"What can I get you, Clara?" Abby said, reaching for the wine glasses. "Red or white?"

"Nothing for me right now, thanks," Clara said.

With everyone here, Abby and the others turned to the table and the selection of nibblies. After loading up their plates, they made their way to the living room and settled in. Though the living room wasn't large, the long sofa and comfortable side chairs offered more than enough seating. The glow of colorful lights from the Christmas tree bathed everyone in a cozy glow.

As was usually the case, the book segment of their Book Club evening was dispensed with in short order — three of the attendees hadn't read the book, which also was usually the case — and conversation turned to catching up, gossip, and laughter. Elsie had just finished sharing the latest goings-on at the community center when her husband Bert stepped into the dining room and surveyed the table offerings with satisfaction.

"Elsie, okay if I help myself?"

"Leave a slice of apple pie for Abby — she hasn't had any yet. Otherwise, have at it."

Bert grinned and grabbed a plate. An energetic man in his sixties with white hair, rosy cheeks, and merry eyes, he looked like Santa's younger, trimmer brother. Tonight he was dressed in coveralls and a red-and-white sweater depicting a smiling snowman with a top hat and corncob pipe.

"Don't mean to interrupt — won't be here but a sec," he said. "Seeing as Luke's still at the bandstand, I'm heading over to lend moral support." He turned to leave, plate in hand, then swiveled back. "But you know, while I'm here, I have a quick question for Abby."

Abby eyed him warily. As the town's mayor, Bert was always on the lookout for opportunities to make life better in Heartsprings Valley, and he had zero qualms about asking folks to pitch in and help out. From the way he leaned forward, Abby knew he was about to hit her up for a favor, most likely something related to —

"It's about the Christmas charity drive," Bert said, finishing her thought.

"What about it, Bert?" Abby said, trying to keep her tone neutral.

"As you know, this year's drive supports local job-training efforts, especially those focusing on the trades. The goal is to help young people and those transitioning from other careers, including the military, to find good-paying jobs in solid, growing industries."

"A worthy and important goal," Abby said.

"Absolutely. One of the nonprofits needs an expert in culinary arts to run a training session on commercial kitchen management."

Abby's brow furrowed. "That's a huge area. Entire programs are devoted to that."

"Understood. The nonprofit is planning something introductory — a class that newcomers can use to dip their toe into the field before enrolling in a certified program. The idea is to help future trainees learn something about an industry they might have an interest in working in professionally."

Abby held Bert's gaze. Despite her reservations about the favor her irrepressible mayor was about to ask of her, she found herself warming to the idea of the course. Back when she'd been preparing to open the chocolate shop, an introduction to professional kitchen management would have been a godsend, if only to open her eyes to the scope and scale of what she needed to master.

"What's the course called?" Abby asked.

"That's up to the person who teaches it," Bert said. "But the nonprofit is thinking about something like 'Introduction to Professional Kitchen Management.'"

Abby slowly exhaled. "And what you're leading up to is...?"

"I think you'd be the perfect person to take the reins."

For a long second, Abby considered her answer before responding. "Bert, thank you for thinking of me. But I'm afraid I just can't. I'm simply overloaded right now."

Hettie Mae nodded vigorously. "Abby, I agree. You are overloaded. But maybe this class can help."

Abby's brow furrowed. "How so?"

"You need help in the kitchen, right?"

"I do, but...."

"And by help, I mean the *right* kind of help, right?"

"Of course...."

"Specifically, you need help from folks who not only *like* making chocolates, but are *good* at making chocolates."

"Yes, and that —"

"That poses a challenge, I know. Because you have high standards. After all, Abby's Chocolate Heaven produces only the very best."

Abby gave Bert a shrug. "Hettie Mae's pretty

much summed it up. Right now, I just don't have the bandwidth to help with the classes."

"Hang on," Clara said, jumping in. "That's not what Hettie Mae is saying."

"Right," Hettie Mae said.

Abby turned to her friend, puzzled. "Then what are you saying?"

Hettie Mae sat up even straighter. "Your lack of bandwidth — listen to me, I sound so high-tech — is exactly why you need to lead those training sessions."

"I'm not following."

"How else are you going to find the right help if you don't go out and find it?"

Abby resisted the urge to shake her head. Her friend had a point, but committing to teach a class on the slim chance of meeting someone who might be the right fit for her kitchen was —

"Besides," Hettie Mae added, interrupting her train of thought, "if the only things you always do are the things you always do, life gets pretty stale pretty fast."

Abby blinked, taken aback. She heard this advice from Hettie Mae a lot — it was one of her favorite refrains — but now, perhaps because of her realization earlier that day about losing steam, the admonition hit home.

"You never know," Clara added. "You might find

a student at the nonprofit with the skill set and interest to help you at the shop."

Abby felt her pulse quicken. What if Clara and Hettie Mae were right?

"I mean, you'll be training them, right?" Clara continued. "That means you can show them how to make chocolates the way you want chocolates to be made. You'll see very quickly which students might be a fit."

"Good point," Gail said approvingly.

Abby allowed the idea to bounce through her head, reluctantly accepting that her friends might be onto something. She took a deep breath. "I have to say, having someone at the shop who knows how to make chocolates the way they need to be made would be a huge help."

"Of course it would," Hettie Mae said. "It'd do you a world of good."

From his spot standing near the dining table, Bert had wisely been remaining silent. Now he cleared his throat. "The next round of training starts in January. Can I tell the nonprofit director to give you a call?"

With five pairs of eyes on her, Abby resisted the urge to sigh. She was fully aware of how skillfully she'd just been maneuvered into agreeing to yet another responsibility.

The real question was: How did she feel about that?

With a smile, she said, "You are incorrigible,

every single one of you. But yes, Bert, you can tell her to give me a call."

"Great," Bert said with a grin and an appreciative nod. "Thank you, Abby." Then, with a wave, he headed out.

Abby turned to the other women. "I'm too easy, aren't I?"

"Way too easy," Elsie said with a smile.

Gail picked up the wine bottle and, without asking, topped up Abby's glass, then turned to Clara.

"You ready now?"

"No thanks, I'm fine," Clara said, choosing that moment to check her phone.

"You sure?" Hettie Mae said, clearly puzzled. Clara was usually good for two glasses, so why no wine tonight?

"Totally sure, all good," Clara said again, her focus on the phone seeming to deepen, like it was suddenly the most fascinating thing on earth.

That's when it hit them. Simultaneously, they *knew*.

A smile appeared on Gail's lips.

Hettie Mae's eyes widened.

Elsie let out a quiet gasp.

"Clara," Abby said carefully. "Any news you and Luke would like to share?"

After a pause, Clara looked up from her phone, her eyes shining. "We're expecting."

The room exploded with cheers.

"Congratulations, Clara!" Abby pulled her in for a hug. "When's the due date?"

"Last week of April."

"That's so wonderful."

"It is wonderful," Clara said, her cheeks flushed. "Also exhilarating and overwhelming and incredible and more than a little terrifying! But scary in a good way, I think? I hope?"

"Of course in a good way!" Elsie said.

"We've just started to tell people. You're among the first to know."

"We're so happy for you," Gail said.

Hettie Mae laughed. "Heartsprings Valley's next generation — coming soon!"

Abby found herself wiping away tears of happiness, already looking forward to the day when she would meet Clara's new bundle of joy.

Change wasn't always bad, she reminded herself as congratulations and laughter flowed through the room.

Sometimes, change could be *wonderful*.

CHAPTER 5

*A*bby had a dream that night, one vivid enough that the memory of it lingered long after she awoke. In the dream, she found herself far away from Heartsprings Valley and far from her little chocolate shop, back at her old job at her old accounting firm, staring blankly at rows of numbers filling her computer screen, in the cubicle that once served as the center of her professional world. A glance past the cubicles through the windows revealed dusk descending and, across the parking lot, trees mostly bare of leaves. It was winter outside. Somehow, even from within her bland, sterile cube, she could feel the coldness in her bones.

Why was she back here, in her old life? If one believed that dreams had meaning, then this dream was probably a message of some sort.

But if so, what? In the dream, she found herself

standing and stretching her shoulders, tired after yet another long day. Though her work wasn't difficult, it wasn't what she wanted to do, and the gradual wear and tear that came from living a life she didn't enjoy was affecting more than just her mood.

She heard a voice call her name. It was the receptionist from the front desk. "Abby, you have a visitor up front."

A visitor? Who could that be? Abby followed the receptionist to the guest lobby.

The instant her eyes landed on the stranger, she realized which day it was.

Trembling with knowledge she hadn't possessed that fateful day, she approached the stranger and said, almost like it was a script that she couldn't alter, "Hi, I'm Abby. Can I help you?"

The stranger, a young woman with a smart, professional appearance, gave her a cheerful smile. "Are you Abby Martin?"

"Yes, I am," Abby replied.

The woman handed her an envelope. "You've been served. Have a nice day."

And with that, the woman turned and left, leaving Abby with astonishment on her face and an envelope in her hand that contained what she'd been half-expecting for weeks now but still wasn't ready for: a petition for divorce.

As the shock rolled through her — and shock it was, despite knowing that this moment was coming

— she sensed that something about her dream was different. Something had changed. Her dream was no longer following the script.

Over her shoulder, she heard a new voice gently calling her name.

Confused, she turned around and found —

Gail?

Yes, her friend was standing there, dressed in a costume that was very un-Gail-like — a head-to-toe Santa suit topped with a festive Santa hat. Some people could pull off the full Santa, but she'd never thought of Gail as one of them.

"Gail," Abby managed to gasp, "what are you doing here?"

"Well," her friend said, considering her question. "I think the first thing I'm here to do is give you a big hug." And with that, she pulled Abby into her arms and whispered softly in her ear, "I'm so sorry you have to relive the pain of this moment. I can only imagine how difficult it must have been to go through what you went through."

Abby allowed the hug to linger. "It would have been so nice to have you here that day. I definitely could have used this hug."

"Did it really happen like we just saw? The woman handing you the divorce papers in your office lobby and then saying, 'Have a nice day'?"

"Yes," Abby said, swallowing back a rush of emotion. "Just like that." She broke away and gazed at her friend. "I don't think I've ever seen you dressed so ... festively."

Gail smiled and did a twirl. "Am I not the essence of the Christmas spirit?"

"Is that what you are?" Abby said doubtfully. "The Christmas spirit?"

"In a way, yes. My job in this dream is to remind you of a turning point in your life."

Abby frowned, unsure what she meant. "A turning point?"

"Not the moment we just experienced, painful and distressing though that was. But rather the turning point that comes next."

Abby felt her heart rate quicken. "Gail, what do you mean?"

"I'm not supposed to say more."

"Why not?"

"It's something you need to remember on your own. Those are the rules."

"The rules? Whose rules?"

Her friend was starting to shimmer, becoming less visible, like a spirit fading away.

"Gail, wait, don't go," Abby said.

"Remember what you did next," Gail said as she vanished. "Remember, Abby — it's important."

And with that, she was gone.

Abby awoke with a start, her heart racing.

She reached out blindly, gasping with relief as her hand closed over her comforter. Thank goodness, she was awake and back in the present day, in her warm bed in her cozy cottage in Heartsprings Valley. A glance at the clock on her nightstand revealed it was just after six. Through the bedroom windows, the sky held a faint hint of the approaching dawn.

She shut her eyes, willing her heart to slow down. What a dream! Most nights, she barely recalled dreaming anything. But this particular vision felt so alive, so real....

She took a deep breath, then exhaled slowly. Her alarm was set to go off in twenty minutes. But there was no way she was getting back to sleep, not in the state she was in. Stifling a groan, she swung her legs out of bed and prepared to confront yet another busy day.

Minutes later, under a cascade of hot water in the shower, she tried to recall exactly what she'd done after being handed the divorce petition. She was pretty sure she hadn't confided in anyone at work — her initial instinct had been to act like nothing significant had happened. After walking back to her cube, she'd shut off her computer, grabbed her handbag, and headed as planned to the grocery store. At first, the familiar routines — driving to the store, pushing a shopping cart up and down the aisles, picking out items, exchanging pleasantries with the checkout clerk — had kept the impact of the divorce petition at bay. But as she pulled into the driveway of the home she'd once shared with her husband, her facade had given way. She'd barely managed to get the groceries inside and on the kitchen counter before angry tears started flowing.

Her husband had moved out a month ago, but part of her had still hoped they could find a way forward. Clearly, that hope was for naught.

So was this how her divorce began? With an impersonal "Have a nice day" from a stranger?

Yes, she answered, letting the tears flow, no longer holding back. Apparently so.

As the shower's warmth flowed over her in the present day, she took a deep breath and shook her head at the memory. The hot water felt so good. She did a lot of her best thinking in the shower, so she might as well put her time here to good use.

The turning point that Santa-suited Gail was urging her to remember — what was it? Perhaps it was the moment in which she finally accepted that her marriage was over? Or perhaps the dream was about something simpler — an affirmation that, every now and then, a good cry was a good thing?

She shook her head, unsatisfied. Why had Gail shown up? Why the guest appearance?

Then she remembered: On the same evening of the divorce petition, she'd spoken with Gail. Her friend had called while Abby was pouring herself a glass of wine from a bottle she'd been saving for a special occasion. The wine was a favorite, a cabernet from a small vineyard in Northern California that she and her husband had visited several years earlier, before the fault lines in their marriage reached the surface. The wine was smooth and complex, with a hint of oak from the barrel. It paired well with grilled meats and also, to her surprise, dark chocolates. On an impulse the previous Christmas, she'd splurged and ordered a dozen bottles. The final bottle now stood open on her dining table, next to a wine glass, ready to play its part in commemorating the significance of this moment.

She picked up the glass and swirled it gently before bringing it to her lips and breathing in the aroma. After a big gulp — too big, but hey, she'd had a day — she was seized with a sudden impulse. With a dash of resolve, she ran to her handbag, grabbed a piece of paper and a pen, returned to her seat at the dining table, and wrote:

Change can be good.
Open your eyes and ears and heart.
Embrace your passion.
You won't regret it.

She stared at the piece of paper, astonished. Had she — the careful, cautious accountant who examined every choice from every angle before deciding anything — actually written those bold words?

At that moment, she was saved from answering by the ringing of her phone. She picked up and was pleased beyond measure to hear Gail on the other end, calling with an update about the small New England town she'd just moved to. Abby listened as Gail filled her in, grateful for the distraction and comforted by the details of her friend's busy new life. It was only when Gail turned the conversation around and asked about her that Abby finally allowed herself to share what had happened. Softly and hesitantly, she told Gail about the petition, gradually allowing her hurt and anger and sadness to flow uninhibited. When Gail insisted that Abby come up for a visit — "this weekend, no arguing" — Abby had allowed herself to be persuaded.

And so it was, a few days later, that Abby found herself staring at the "Retail Space Available" sign in the display window of the vacant store on Heartsprings Valley's town square. The words she'd written in her moment of resolve leapt to mind. Ever-alert, Gail had noticed the flush of excitement on Abby's cheeks and immediately arranged for Abby to check out the space. One look was all it took: The instant Abby stepped into the tiny kitchen in the back of the store, she'd known what she was going to do.

With a sigh, Abby turned off the shower and reached for her towel. That had been eight years ago. She had no regrets about the chance she'd taken in uprooting herself, leaving her secure job, and pursuing her passion for chocolates in a town she barely knew. There had been plenty of anxious moments in the years since — starting a small business meant endless amounts of hard work, with risk and uncertainty her constant companions — but she'd pushed through the difficulties, found her footing, and made it work. She had every reason to be proud.

Maybe that's what the dream was telling her? To have pride in what she'd accomplished? Or was it about what she'd chosen to do in her moment of crisis — throwing caution to the wind and moving up here?

She was probably overthinking this, she realized. So what if she'd remembered a dream? People remembered their dreams all the time. Most of the time, there was no greater underlying cosmic significance.

Most of the time, a dream was just a dream.

CHAPTER 6

*T*he next few days zoomed by in a frenetic blur. With Christmas fast approaching, customers poured into Abby's little shop and even more called or hopped online to place orders. For three nights in a row, she worked late into the evening, making batch after batch of chocolates to keep pace with the demand.

Almost before she knew it, the day of John's first private lesson arrived. Throughout the week, she'd done her best to avoid thinking too much about the lesson, which hadn't been easy. His request had been a surprise, and surprises were rare in her structured existence, especially during this time of the year, when her every waking moment was devoted to keeping her head above water.

During a blessed moment of quiet, she allowed herself to rewind to their brief encounter. Not only was his request surprising, it was charming. His wish for a shared hobby with Maggie had warmed her heart.

Plus — and it was best to openly admit this and not shy away from it — she'd felt something when they shook hands. She didn't want to characterize that something, because there really was no point in doing that. No matter what she might choose to call "it" — the spark, the connection, the sense of possibility she'd felt — the simple truth was that "it" was but a moment in time which meant little and would almost certainly lead to nothing. John was a widower with two kids and a career, and she was a chocolatier who'd agreed to give him private lessons. That was the deal. Nothing less, and certainly nothing more.

Still, she acknowledged, the "it" she'd felt wasn't completely without value. It was probably helpful and good to think of "it" as a reminder that life could be about more than just work, if one allowed oneself that option.

She exhaled deeply, wishing she weren't so good at twisting herself into emotional knots. *Sometimes, a handshake is just a handshake. Stop overthinking everything.* She turned her attention to her kitchen, trying to figure out what she was forgetting, her gaze quickly roaming over the tiny space. From where she was standing next to the swinging doors leading to the front room, she could practically see every inch of her workspace: the galley-style layout, the walk-through pantry, and beyond that the tiny two-piece bathroom next to the cramped mudroom by the back door. Aside from the stainless steel refrigerator, her appliances — oven, microwave, dishwasher, blast cooler, and second small fridge — were tucked beneath the marble countertops she'd installed on both sides of the galley when she moved in. An industrial sink interrupted the countertop on one wall, and the stove's six burners did the same on the other. A row of upper cabinets on the oven wall completed the layout.

Her color scheme was good — veined gray-and-white countertops, white cabinets, and blue-grey tile for the backsplash — and the lighting was warm and more than adequate.

But what I'd give for more room. Oh, to have more counter space. And an island with a big countertop!

She shook her head, getting irritated with herself. *Yet another wish she didn't have time for right now.* Turning to her preparations, she eyed the ingredients lined up on the counter and confirmed she was ready to go. She'd be teaching John how to make salted caramels this evening. Not only were they among the easier pieces to make, they were her most popular item and she was running low. Through the kitchen's tiny back window, she spied a dusting of white on the window ledge, sparkling in the kitchen's reflected light. The snowfall the other night had been lighter than expected, but another round was due in a couple of days.

A glance at the wall clock above the swinging doors told her it was almost seven. John was due any moment. Anxiety fluttered through her. Why was she feeling so nervous? She'd led dozens of classes over the years. John was just her newest student. She would enjoy teaching him — she always enjoyed showing others how to make chocolates. There was something so gratifying about witnessing the dawning of comprehension in her students' eyes when they learned how a piece of chocolate gets made. Even better was the moment when they realized that making them was something *they* could do. Chocolate-making wasn't just for big companies or trained experts: It was a skill, an activity, that anyone could learn if they brought their passion and commitment to the task.

Up front, the shop bell rang. She stepped through the swinging doors and found John shutting the shop door behind him.

"Evening, Abby," he said, his gaze holding hers.

"Evening, John," she replied.

He came across like he had a few days earlier — handsome and trim, confident with perhaps a hint of nervousness, dressed in jeans, with a dark-blue button-down collared shirt beneath his blue winter coat.

Briefly, her mind went to her own appearance

— she'd spent more time than usual on her hair and makeup this morning, and just minutes earlier had been at the mirror for a final touchup — before she hurriedly pushed all such thoughts aside and said, in a voice that pleased her with its steadiness, "Ready for an evening of chocolate, chocolate, and more chocolate?"

He grinned. "Let's do it." He gestured to his coat. "Where should I...?"

"Back here."

He followed her through the galley kitchen to the back door, where she pointed to a row of hooks. "Hang up your stuff, wash your hands, and we'll get started."

"Thanks." As he eased past her to the sink to soap up, she was struck anew by how tiny her kitchen was and how narrow the galley layout suddenly seemed. He was a good half-foot taller than her, which was part of it — he seemed too big for the space. How was it going to work with both of them in here? Her kitchen could handle one person, but two?

"How's your week been?" he said as he scrubbed up. "Busy?"

"Oh, definitely. Pretty much nonstop. Christmas is always the craziest time of the year."

"I really appreciate you squeezing in these lessons."

"I was happy to, especially given the reason. Your kids are adorable."

"That they are." He finished rinsing and grabbed a hand towel hanging next to the sink.

"How was the hike, by the way?"

"Really good. A beautiful day. And the trail wasn't steep at all — Mom and Dad handled it just fine. The view of Heartsprings Lake is spectacular."

"It's one of my favorite walks."

His gaze wandered over the walls and ceiling of the tiny kitchen. "Your kitchen is quite … cozy."

She nodded. "If by 'cozy' you mean way too small and way too tight, then I completely agree."

"I guess I do mean that," he said with a chuckle. "Is this where you make your chocolates?"

"Mostly, yes. A few winters ago, a water pipe burst during a big freeze and I had to temporarily relocate to the rec center and use their kitchen — the same kitchen we'll be using for the class with the kids in two weekends, by the way. Sometimes I make chocolates at home, though my kitchen there isn't much bigger."

"Which means most of the time, you're right here."

"That's right."

"This is where the magic happens."

She smiled. "Well, there's nothing magical about making good chocolates, as I plan to show you tonight. All you need are the right ingredients, combined together the right way."

"Guess we'll see if I can meet the challenge. By

the way, the kids loved that marshmallow-cherry piece."

"Glad to hear."

"And the one I picked out — the dark chocolate with coffee? That piece was actually really special."

Abby felt a glow at his words. The chocolate he'd chosen was her new favorite. "Special in what way? I'm not fishing for compliments, by the way — I want to be clear about that. It's one of my newer pieces. I'm curious how you describe it."

He paused, considering. "Not sure I have the vocabulary, but I'll give it a shot." He rubbed his hands together. "But first, some context, to let you know where I'm coming from. When it comes to candy bars and chocolates and the like, I'm not picky. Most of the time, I'm good with regular stuff — you know, like a chocolate bar from the grocery store or gas station. I'll be filling the tank and grab a bar for the ride home or wherever, and that really hits the spot."

"I can relate," Abby said. "Though in my case, my go-to comfort snack usually involves apples."

His eyebrows rose. "Apples?"

"Pretty much every way you can think of them being made."

"Plain old apples?"

"Nothing like a fresh, crisp bite."

"Apple pie?"

"I love apple pie."

"Even more than cherry and blueberry and pumpkin and…?"

"I enjoy those, too. But I don't think I've ever had an apple pie or crisp or turnover I haven't enjoyed."

"A bold statement," he said with a grin.

"One I stand by," she replied, grinning along with him.

"Even those mass-produced apple whatevers you get at the gas station?"

"Even those."

His eyebrows rose. "In my experience, some of those are…."

"Surprisingly satisfying," she said firmly, unwilling to concede that he might have a point. Over the years, she'd bitten into more than a few of those factory-made, individually wrapped items, plucked from the back of a neglected store shelf, that were well past their sell-by date….

"Well," he said, "you've never had an apple pie made by me."

Her brow furrowed. "Why would I not enjoy an apple pie made by you?"

"To be honest, I've never made one. But I'm pretty sure I'd mess it up. I'm hopeless in the kitchen. A walking disaster zone. Maybe even cursed."

"You mentioned that the other day. But come on — a disaster?"

"Category 5. I wish I was exaggerating."

"I'm sure you're doing just that. The kids seem healthy enough. Clearly they're being, um, *fed*."

He laughed. "Okay, maybe I'm exaggerating a little. I have a decent handle on breakfast — oatmeal, cereal, toast, pancakes, even bacon and eggs — and for lunch I can put together a sandwich. But dinner, not so much. I know how to make four dishes. Mom cooks for us one night, and the other two nights we eat out."

"Four dishes? That's a beginning."

"The beginning and the end. Everything else I try ends in disaster."

Abby smiled at him. "I find that hard to believe."

"I have proof."

"Proof?"

"Photographic evidence." He pulled out his phone and flipped through his photos until he found the ones he was after. "The full scale of the catastrophe — immortalized forever."

Her eyes widened as she gazed upon a photo of a blackened turkey carcass. The poor bird was beyond charred — it looked like it had been dragged into the desert and left to die of thirst in the scorching sun, then tossed into a raging bonfire and run over with a tractor for good measure.

"Don't tell me this was Thanksgiving."

"A total disaster."

"What happened?"

"We'd just moved up here, and I wasn't familiar with the oven."

A suspicion came to her. "Don't tell me…."

"The self-cleaning setting."

She gasped. "Oh, no."

"Oh, yes."

"You couldn't open the oven?"

"It wouldn't let me open it until it was done cleaning."

"How long was the turkey trapped in there?"

"Far too long."

"What did you do?"

"At a certain point, the bird started smoking."

"Oh, no!"

"We had to open the doors and windows to air out the house. The fire alarms were going off. We had to bring in a ladder and turn them all off."

"What did you end up doing, once you finally got the oven open again?"

"Let's just say Thanksgiving ended up being burgers and hot dogs."

"Oh, no!"

"I mean, we still had mashed potatoes and stuffing and cranberry and apple pie and what-not — all of which came premade from the grocery store, by the way — but Thanksgiving without a turkey…."

"You poor thing."

"The kids never miss a chance to rib me about it.

'The Thanksgiving Day Turkey Disaster' has entered the family lore."

Abby laughed. She was glad he recognized the humor in the situation, though she could only imagine how stressful it must have been at the time.

"You know, one bad day doesn't mean you're a disaster in the kitchen. Every cook, every baker, has stories of their own to tell."

"Ah, but I'm not done." He flipped to another photo, showing what appeared to be a burnt slab of *something* in a casserole dish.

"What is that?" Abby said, squinting as she zoomed in.

"It was supposed to be lasagna."

Lasagna? The substance in the dish looked like *charcoal*. Abby bit her lip. She couldn't let herself laugh — that would be rude.

"I'm ... sorry," she managed to say with a straight face.

"I forgot to turn on the timer."

"So it...."

"Baked and baked and baked and...."

"That poor lasagna...."

He gazed at her, amusement in his eyes. "It's okay to laugh, by the way."

A grin broke through. "I'm sorry. I really am. But those pictures...."

"Are atrocious. I could also tell you about the time I made pumpkin pie using salt instead of sugar

— and the expression on the kids' faces when they dug in — but I think you begin to get the picture."

Salt instead of sugar? Abby bit her lip to keep from smiling. "What are the four dishes you know how to make?"

"Spaghetti is the one I know best."

"Always a good one to have handy."

"I can make breaded chicken with mashed potatoes and green beans."

"That sounds nice…."

"I can make beef stroganoff."

"Mmm, I love that one."

"And when I don't burn it to a crisp, I know how to make lasagna."

He gazed at her expectantly, as if awaiting her judgment.

Abby took a deep breath, then said, "I know people who can't even boil water. Your dishes are on the easy side, but they all require a basic level of competence."

A smile came to his lips. "Are you saying I'm not a lost cause?"

"There's hope for you yet."

"We'll see what you say after tonight's lesson. But about your chocolate piece," he said, returning to their earlier topic. "Now that you know the context — me the walking, talking culinary danger zone — I can try to tell you why I enjoyed it."

"Context duly noted," she said with a smile.

He paused to collect his thoughts. "I enjoyed it because it *wasn't* like the candy bars I get in the store. It had a sharpness that surprised me. The chocolate was rich, the coffee had depth, and there was something else in there too, an ingredient I couldn't put my finger on...."

"Cardamom," Abby said.

"What's that?"

"It's a spice, originally from India, quite aromatic, with an intense taste."

"Interesting," he said, considering. "Maybe that's why I didn't feel an urge to gobble it down all at once. Instead, I found myself lingering, taking my time. Each small bite seemed to mean something."

He gets it, she thought, her heart beating faster. Somehow, this culinary neophyte understood what she'd been aiming for.

"Thank you. I'm glad to hear that. That particular piece is actually an experiment of sorts."

"How so?"

"Most of my chocolates are aimed at a wider audience. I pay attention to what my customers like and do my best to make them happy. For example, the salted caramels we'll be making tonight are easily my most popular."

"The coffee-cardamom piece doesn't follow that playbook?"

"It's more of a specialty taste. It's more to *my* taste. It has less sugar, for one thing — hence the sharpness — and combines ingredients in a way that most folks aren't used to."

"So it's a departure of sorts."

"It is."

"Does this mean you're branching out? Expanding your business?"

She paused before answering. The idea of *expanding* seemed to resonate with her somehow. "I'd like to, someday."

He was nodding. "A new line of chocolates aimed at connoisseurs?"

"Yes," she said, surprising herself. Aside from briefly mentioning the idea to Gail and a couple of others, she hadn't shared the possibility with much of anyone. Yet she'd done just that with John, who was basically a stranger.

Still, she decided, she felt comfortable with him. He seemed thoughtful and attentive. Perhaps it was the kindness she sensed in his brown eyes….

She blinked. *What was she doing?*

"So," she said, clapping her hands together to bring herself back to reality, "we should get to work."

"Yes," he said, "let's get to work. Even though I have no idea what that means."

CHAPTER 7

*A*bby smiled. "It means we start by making sure our hands and the countertop and bowls and utensils are completely clean."

John held his hands out. "Freshly scrubbed."

"Excellent. Before you got here, I cleaned our workspace and utensils, so we're covered there. The reason I begin every lesson by emphasizing cleanliness is its importance for chocolates. Even a stray drop of water can cause chocolate to seize up."

"Seize up?" John asked.

"Basically, chocolate and water don't get along. Water will turn lovely smooth melted chocolate into a pasty mess."

"I had no idea."

"Also, in terms of cleanliness, the last thing you want to encounter when you bite into a chocolate is something that's not supposed to be there."

"Like a hair?" he said, his face scrunching up.

"Or worse."

"Yikes. Okay, I'm sold. Clean is important. Clean is essential."

"Good," she said. "The second point I emphasize is safety. Hot caramel, for example, sticks and burns if you get it on you. Safety is always our first priority."

"Got it."

"Speaking of, your first step: Grab the double boiler, fill the bottom pot with a couple inches of water, set it on the stove, and turn on the heat."

She watched him figure out which pot to use — he hesitated, but only for a second. Then he brought it to the sink, added water, set it on a burner, and switched on the gas.

As the flame gently whooshed to life, he turned toward her, seeking confirmation. "Like this?"

"I knew you knew how to boil water."

"Ha."

"Keep your eye on it. When it starts boiling, turn off the heat and set the upper pot on top."

"What's the hot water for?"

"It's the heat source we'll use to melt the chocolate. The temperatures we're after for the chocolate are well below boiling. Hence the use of the double boiler."

He nodded. "Like radiant floor heating."

She blinked, surprised by the reference. "Is that so?"

"Same technique. When it's run under the floor, the tubes of hot water give off a heat that rises gently through the floor to keep your toes toasty warm."

"I heard you're an architect?"

"Residential mostly, but also small workspaces."

"Any projects around here?"

"Right now, I'm finishing up a project just outside town."

"What kind of project?"

"A workspace."

Even as the words left his mouth, she realized she knew exactly which workspace it was and found herself appreciating what she guessed was his natural discretion. He could have chosen that moment to reveal — to brag about — the famous client he was working for. But he hadn't.

Still, since she already knew.... "Any chance this workspace is up on Heartsprings Ridge and intended as a woodworking and furniture studio?"

"Ah," he said with a grin. "So you know."

"James and Melody are friends."

"Should have figured. Folks around here all seem to know each other."

"Not always and not everyone, but what you say is true more often than not."

"I'm still re-adjusting. I grew up in Eagle Cove

but moved away for college and ended up living in Boston for twenty years. I'm still in the process of recalibrating the internal programming."

"Recalibrating how?"

"Back to 'small-town' mode. In Boston, when I met new people, chances were our social circles didn't overlap. They had their crowd and I had mine, and ne'er the twain had met."

"But here in Heartsprings Valley…."

"The opposite. Take you and me. Until a few days ago, we were strangers. But I bet you and I know a bunch of people in common, and not just James and Melody."

"I'm sure you're right. And I agree, it does take a bit of time to adjust."

She glanced at the wall clock — goodness, time was flying. "Okay, we need to focus. The caramels won't make themselves." She pointed to the marble countertop. "Here's where we'll be tempering the chocolate. For this step, it's best to use a clean, cool surface, like this marble."

His brow furrowed. "Tempering — does the term refer to temperature?"

She nodded. "At a basic level, it means heating and then cooling the chocolate to get it ready for use. Tempering changes the chocolate — it helps keep the chocolate from melting when you touch it, and gives the chocolate a glossy and smooth finish."

"When you say it changes the chocolate, what do you mean?"

"As heat is applied, the cocoa butter in the chocolate melts. Then, as the cocoa butter cools, it crystalizes." She pointed to the utensils lined up on the counter. "Time to get to know your chocolate thermometer."

He turned toward the counter. "The ice pick with buttons on the handle?"

"The very one."

He picked it up and examined it. "This little guy...."

"Is your new best friend. You'll be using it to make sure you're heating and cooling the chocolate to the right temperatures."

"What happens if we apply the wrong temperatures?"

"Long story short? The chocolate can be ruined."

His eyebrows rose. "Ruined?"

"For use in making chocolate pieces, yes."

"Wow." He returned the thermometer to the counter. "So there's precision required."

"Most definitely."

"Pressure's on," he said with a grin.

"In all seriousness, I don't want you worrying about ruining a batch of chocolate. I've done it myself countless times. Every chocolatier will tell you the same. In most cases, the chocolate is still usable as an ingredient for cakes or sauces."

"Do you make cakes?"

"Once in a while, yes, I get asked to make chocolate cakes or brownies or cookies, usually for parties or catered events. It makes for a nice change of pace, but baking isn't a focus for me."

He glanced at the stove. "Water's boiling." Quickly, he slipped past her, turned off the burner, and set the upper pot on top.

As he returned to his earlier spot, his arm brushed hers, and she found herself confronting two unwanted thoughts:

Her tiny kitchen was way too small.

And:

She liked being close to him. He had a nice energy — he moved with confidence. And he smelled clean — a hint of soap mixed with a dash of aftershave.

With dismay, she realized where her thoughts were heading. *No good!*

John, bless his oblivious heart, hadn't noticed. His gaze was on the marble counter. "Are we making the chocolate before we temper it?"

Gratefully, she turned her attention to his question. "Not tonight, no. For some of my chocolate pieces, I make the chocolate from scratch — I'm always interested in testing out new flavors — but there's no time for that this evening. Also, the chocolate I use for the caramels comes from a specialty maker."

She opened the refrigerator and took out two big blocks of dark chocolate.

He stared at the blocks, his gaze thoughtful. "I suppose there are a million ways to make chocolate."

"The variations are endless."

"How do you know which variation to go with?"

"That," she said, "is a very good question. For me, it's a matter of taste and experience and intuition, with lots of trial-and-error thrown in for good measure."

"What do you like about this particular chocolate?"

"It's a dark milk chocolate — close to dark, but with just the right amount of milk — which gives it a rich smoothness. There's depth to it, but the dash of milk takes the edge off the sharpness. And it pairs beautifully with the caramel and sea salt."

At that moment, they heard the ring of the front door's bell.

"A customer." She handed him the chocolate blocks, reached below the counter, pulled out a cutting board, and set it on the counter. "While I'm up front, I want you to chop the two chocolate blocks into small chunks."

"How big should the chunks be?"

"About half an inch square."

As she turned, she caught the sudden anxiety in his eyes.

"You can do this." She pointed to the utensils. "Use that big knife. Don't worry if the chunks aren't exactly the same size."

"Okay," he said doubtfully.

"Holler when you're done. Back in a sec."

CHAPTER 8

The mild panic on John's face was an expression Abby was familiar with — many of her students reacted the same way upon realizing that *they* and not Abby were actually going to be the ones making the chocolates. As she helped the customer up front with her purchase — three boxes, plus a few individual pieces she simply couldn't resist — she heard John getting to work, the solid *thunk* of the knife on the cutting board carrying into the front room.

Seconds after the customer headed out the door, purchases in hand, John popped his head through the swinging doors. "I think I did it."

Abby bustled in. A quick glance confirmed he'd gotten it mostly right. "Good. Give those bigger chunks there a couple more chops and we'll be ready for our next step."

He did as ordered. "Folks still shopping at this hour? Is it like this every night?"

"This time of year, yes. We might be interrupted a few times more."

"I'm grateful you agreed to do these lessons."

"It's for a good cause," she said with a smile. "And now you already added a new skill to your kitchen repertoire: chocolate chopping."

"Ha. Okay, what now?"

"Take two thirds of the chocolate and set it in the upper pot of the double boiler."

"Two thirds? Should I measure it out?"

"No, just eyeball it."

She watched him separate the chocolate on the cutting board into three roughly equal piles and add two piles to the pot. He worked with concentration, his attention focused on the task at hand.

"Good," she said. "Now, for the next step, you'll need a soft spatula and the chocolate thermometer."

From the counter, he found what he needed. "I'm guessing I stir the chocolate to help it melt, and check the temperature while I do so?"

"That's right." So far, John was proving a quick study. "To ensure the chocolate melts smoothly, stir slowly but thoroughly. The temperature we want is exactly 115 degrees Fahrenheit."

"Exactly?"

"The ideal temperature varies depending on the

chocolate. For this one, I've learned through experience that 115 is better than 114 and better than 116."

"Does the ideal temperature depend on the amount of cocoa butter in the chocolate?"

"Gold star for you."

He smiled. "What do I do when the temperature reaches 115 degrees?"

"Add in the final third, then repeat the stirring and temperature-checking until you're back to 115 degrees."

"And then?"

"Take the chocolate off the boiler and set the pot on a towel on the counter to begin cooling."

John turned his attention to the chocolate melting in the pot. "Something you said earlier...," he said as he stirred.

"What's that?"

"You mentioned needing to adjust to Heartsprings Valley. I take it you're not from around here?"

"I moved here eight years ago."

"What prompted the move? Was it to open the shop?"

She paused, tempted to share more than she usually did, before going with her usual answer. "My friend Gail — she's a veterinarian — had just moved here to join a veterinary practice, and she said I simply had to come up for a visit. When I did, I instantly fell in love with the town. And when I found out that this space was available…."

"Heartsprings Valley has a way of pulling you in, doesn't it? It's pretty special. The kids have adjusted well."

"They seem really great."

"They are." He gave her a wry grin. "At least most of the time."

She chuckled. "They have their moments?"

"Oh, yeah." His grin grew wider. "Let's just say they know how to push each other's buttons."

"Wait till they figure out how to join forces and turn their combined powers on Dad."

"Too late for that. They mastered that move ages ago."

"Oh, dear."

"I have the battle scars to prove it."

She gave him a quick once-over. "Nothing visible, at least that I can see. You seem to have held up pretty well."

Indeed, she realized as the words left her mouth, he'd held up *very* well. His hair was thick and full, tinted with grey but still mostly brown. He carried himself upright and with energy — like he preferred to keep moving instead of standing still.

What are you doing? she asked herself. *Stop it!*

"They're good kids," he said. "They definitely keep me on my toes."

She was about to ask more when the ring of her

phone interrupted them. She reached into her pocket and pulled out her phone.

"It's James — Melody's husband. Okay if I pick up?"

"Absolutely."

She stepped closer to examine the melting chocolate and was pleased by what she saw. "Remember, check the temperature," she said, then hit the button on the phone. "Hello, James."

"Abby," James said, his voice clear despite the cross-country distance. "Glad I reached you."

"You still in L.A.?"

"For the next ten days. We fly back two Saturdays from now."

Abby already knew this, but James didn't know she knew — just like he didn't know about the surprise Melody was planning for him. "What's up?"

"Well," he said, pausing. "I'm planning a little surprise for Melody and I'm hoping I can ask for your help."

Abby went still. *James* was planning a surprise for *Melody*? "You're planning a surprise for Melody?" she repeated out loud.

John turned toward her, puzzled.

"That's right," James said. "It turns out the new furniture workshop is gonna be finished ahead of schedule. So I'm thinking it'd be great to host a little gathering there two Sundays from now — as a surprise — to celebrate the wrap of Melody's new movie."

Abby bit her lip to keep from smiling. Really, this whole thing was adorable. James and Melody both wanted to throw a surprise party for each other, at the same place, on the same day?

And neither knew it?

"James," she said, "I'd be happy to help out. What do you need?"

"A cake. You remember that delicious double-chocolate cake you made for that dinner party?"

"Of course."

"Melody's still raving about it — she loves that cake, says it's the best chocolate cake she's ever had. So I'm thinking it'd be great to have that, with some kind of message on top. You know, like, 'Congrats, that's a wrap!' or something movie-ish?"

"That sounds lovely." After a pause, she added, "Are you doing all the organizing from out there in L.A.?"

"I'm trying to, but I'm gonna call John — he's the architect for the workshop, great guy — and see if I can rope him into helping."

"Ah," Abby said, a grin on her face, her eyes on John. Out loud, she repeated, "So you'll be calling John to see if he's open to helping you organize the surprise party for Melody."

"Yep."

"The surprise at your workshop in two Sundays.

To celebrate the wrap of her new movie."

"Yep, that's it."

The grin on John's face grew wider as the implications sank in.

"Well," Abby said, "I'll be happy to help out with the cake, of course."

"Awesome. Thank you. You'll be able to attend the party, too, right?"

"Of course. Wouldn't miss it for the world."

"I really appreciate this, Abby. Talk with you soon."

And he was gone.

Abby set down the phone and turned to John.

"So…" John said slowly. "Let me see if I got this right. Melody is throwing a surprise party for James to celebrate the opening of his new furniture workshop. And James is throwing a surprise party for Melody to celebrate the end of her new movie."

"That's right."

"The parties are on the same day and at the same location."

"Yes."

"And neither knows what the other is doing."

Abby laughed. "Yes."

"This is gonna be fun," he said, his eyes twinkling. "Can I count on you to help out?"

"Of course," she said immediately, without even a second's hesitation, caught up in the same sense of excitement. "Count me in."

CHAPTER 9

*F*or the next few minutes, chocolate-making was forgotten as Abby found herself telling John the story of how she'd met Melody. In turn, John told her about getting hired by James and Melody to build the furniture workshop.

"They called me the day they got back from their honeymoon," he said. "From the very start, as we brainstormed what we wanted to build, it became clear we were completely in sync. I assume you're familiar with the furniture James makes?"

"Absolutely."

"He has a gift with wood. His pieces are stunning. And with folks starting to discover that, orders are pouring in."

"I hear he's extremely busy."

"The sooner he can get into the workshop and put the space to good use, the better."

"I haven't seen the workshop yet," Abby said. "What's it like?"

"It's large and open, airy and bright, situated across the meadow from the main house. You don't see it when you're driving up. It's kind of nestled in the woods. The back half of the building is devoted to furniture-making and the front area is for display, packing, and shipping."

"The display area — is that so potential clients can see samples?"

"That's the idea. He's already had clients visit Heartsprings Valley to check out his furniture first-hand."

"How big is the space?"

"Pretty big. We built anticipating future growth."

"So the space isn't just for him?"

"We spent a lot of time working through that. Right now, he's a one-man operation. But the influx in orders means he has months of work ahead of him just to catch up. He's considering bringing in folks to help."

"You designed the space to enable that."

He nodded. "We spend so much of our lives at our jobs. It's important to get our workplaces right. We walked through workflow in detail — in his case, the steps involved in turning unfinished pieces of wood into finished furniture — to make sure we placed the right machinery in the right places."

"So the table where he cuts the wood...."

"Is next to the spot where he stacks the cut pieces in preparation for sanding. And so on."

Abby found herself nodding. "That sounds really great. When I think of architecture, I guess I don't think of workflow as much as I do the building itself — the foundations and walls and roofs and windows."

He smiled. "Still essential, all of them. But my role, as I see it, is to create spaces that work in every way — physically, functionally, financially, and emotionally."

"Emotionally?"

"The feeling of a house or workspace is as important, in my view, as its financial and functional requirements."

As he repeated the word "financial," Abby involuntarily glanced at the leaky kitchen window. "I assume the financial aspect covers both construction costs and ongoing expenses?"

John followed her gaze to the window. "Let me guess. In the winter, your heating bill goes through the roof."

She nodded. "The window isn't tight in the frame. It rattles when it's windy. There are days I can almost feel a cold breeze."

"I could help with that."

"I've got it covered, thanks. James has offered to replace the window when I'm ready. But things like that make me mindful of ongoing costs."

His eyes were still on the window. "A good double-pane window can make a world of difference when it comes to basics like energy usage and temperature control. There's other stuff, too. Some exciting new features are becoming affordable for smaller buildings."

"Give me an example," Abby said, intrigued. "Anything you're using in James's new space?"

"Well," he said, considering. "Let's start with energy. The workshop's hooked up to the electrical grid, but we sited the building and designed the roof to capture as much solar energy as possible. The solar energy is converted into electricity to power the equipment and lighting and to heat the water in the radiant piping in the floors and walls. On most days from late spring to early fall, the building will capture enough energy to send electricity to the grid instead of the other way around."

"The seasons are a factor up here, I'm guessing?"

He nodded. "Geography and seasons and weather are always key factors for solar — the amount of sunlight you get determines how much energy you can capture. But the other big factor is the technology, which keeps getting better. Solar costs less than it used to, and it captures more energy than it used to."

"Which means the equation is changing...."

"For the better. We're getting closer to the day

when solar becomes standard for the majority of new building construction."

She liked listening to him talk about his profession, she realized, despite not knowing much about solar energy or home construction. His passion shone through. The way his eyes lit up and his gestures grew more animated....

"You like what you do," she said. "It shows in how you talk about it."

He shot her a grin. "Don't get me started about recent advances in insulation — you'll never shut me up."

Abby laughed. "I'm the same when it comes to chocolates. I've had friends — very good friends, mind you — pull me aside and very gently tell me to zip it."

He was gazing at her intently, with an expression of curiosity and interest that he wasn't trying to hide. He was so easy to talk with — fun, lively, comfortable....

But they weren't on a date, she reminded herself. The point of the two of them spending time together in her tiny kitchen on a Wednesday evening was *not* to get to know each other. The point was to teach him how to make chocolates so that he and his daughter could share a hobby. A glance at the wall clock confirmed that time was flying — and they still had chocolate to temper, caramel to make, molds to fill, and more.

Reluctantly but firmly, Abby shifted their focus back to the lesson, and the chocolate-making continued, though with interruptions from a steady stream of customers popping into the store. During a couple of key moments, Abby had to leave John alone in the kitchen to fend for himself.

The caramels they ended up with weren't up to her usual exacting standard, but they were perfectly acceptable in taste and appearance. John had demonstrated real potential in the kitchen — he paid attention, learned quickly, and executed his tasks skillfully. He probably wasn't destined to become a master chef — his passions were for his architectural work and his family — but Abby sensed a potential for culinary competency that would serve him and his family well.

"So how do they taste?" John asked as he watched her take a bite of a finished piece.

She allowed the flavors to roll over her tongue. "Quite good. Congratulations. You'd never know that a 'walking, talking culinary danger zone' made these."

He laughed, relieved. "I passed?"

"With flying colors. You should feel very pleased with how these turned out."

His gaze lingered on her for a long second. Clearly, he was enjoying spending time with her. Then he blinked, as if realizing something. His cheeks flushed and he glanced at his watch. "Whoa, we're over time."

"Time flies when…."

"When you're having fun." He paused again, as if unwilling to let the moment go. "I'll help you clean up."

"No need for that," she said firmly.

"Hey, I may be a disaster at cooking, but I'm an ace at cleaning."

She smiled. "Is that so?"

He nodded vigorously. "Tons of practice. In the Buckley household, cleanliness is a never-ending quest."

"I can handle the cleanup, I promise. You're the student here, which also makes you the guest. You should get yourself home."

He shook his head. "Nonsense." Without waiting for a reply, he grabbed the caramel pot, turned on the faucet, and started rinsing.

Abby accepted his help with a smile. "Thank you."

They worked in silence for a moment, as if conscious of the possibility that their shared effort might be about more than just cleaning up a kitchen after a chocolate lesson.

"Listen," he said, "about the double-surprise party. I know this is your busy season, so I can handle it."

"I'm happy to lend a hand."

"Are you sure?" His expression was hard to read, but if Abby had to guess, she would've been willing to bet that he felt obligated to offer her an escape hatch but was very much hoping she wouldn't leap through it.

"Positive. I'm sure you'll have questions as you get everything lined up."

"You mean, questions about the catering and decorating and inviting the guests and...."

"All of that. Give me a call or swing by anytime if you'd like my input."

"I'll do that, thanks."

Abby threw a quick glance around the kitchen — most of the cleanup was done. "And on that note, I must insist: Time for you to get home."

He nodded, gave his hands a quick rinse, then retrieved his coat from the rack at the back door. "This was really great, Abby," he said as he buttoned up, his gaze on her. "I can't wait for Lesson Two."

"I had fun," she said, realizing as she said it how much she meant it.

She followed him up to the front. He paused at the door. "Thanks again for everything. I'll see you soon?"

"See you soon."

As she watched him step out into the crisp dark night, her heart beating more rapidly than it had in ages, she found herself wishing their next lesson could begin right away.

CHAPTER 10

a second vivid dream came to Abby that night, one even more surprising and puzzling than the dream a few nights earlier. In her new vision, she found herself in Heartsprings Valley's town square on a bright winter morning, bundled up against the cold in a thick coat and scarf and gloves. The air was crisp. Sunlight glistened off the snowy ground. All around her, snowmen, snow-women, snow-kids, and snow-animals were smiling at her. She found herself grinning back at one particularly adorable snow-dog — a golden retriever, she guessed — who almost seemed to be begging for a game of catch.

The dream felt so *real*. She could almost feel the breeze against her cheeks, which she bet were pink from the cold.

Was this a memory, a moment pulled from her

past, like the dream she'd had the other night? Or was it something else?

The question was rolling through her head when she caught movement among the snowpeople. A flash of red and white.

And then, quite dramatically, the red-and-white flash dashed forward and revealed itself as — Hettie Mae in a full-on Santa suit!

"Morning, Abby!" her friend said as she pulled her in for a quick hug.

"Hettie Mae," Abby gasped. "What's going on?"

Hettie Mae didn't reply. Instead, she let go of Abby and stepped back to pose in her costume, clearly pleased with her getup. "Not my usual style," she said, twirling and laughing. "But I'm enjoying myself, so why not?"

"Hettie Mae, what are you doing here?"

"I'm a manifestation of the Christmas spirit, apparently. At least, that's how I interpret it."

"What do you mean, 'how you interpret it'?"

"We've been asked to help out, but it's not like we've been given an instruction manual."

"Wait," Abby said, trying to follow — there was a lot to unpack in that short statement. "We? Instruction manual? Asked by whom?"

Hettie Mae waved the question away. "Sorry, no time. We have somewhere to be." She stepped forward and slipped her arm through Abby's. "Hold on."

Effortlessly, their feet left the ground and Abby gasped.

They were flying!

Before she could even blink, they were rising high above Heartsprings Valley. Below them, the town sparkled in the bright morning light, the sun glistening off the fresh-fallen snow. Wind rushed through her hair. From below, Abby caught the faint honk of a car horn. As they swung over the lake, Abby spied a gaggle of kids skating energetically on the ice. The higher they soared, the more the town started to resemble Becca's expertly rendered gingerbread houses — the people toy-like, the buildings temptingly delicious.

"Hungry yet?" Hettie Mae said.

Abby couldn't help herself — she laughed. "How did you know I was thinking that?"

"This is a dream, Abby. The usual rules don't apply."

Hettie Mae aimed them over the main road running through the spine of the valley. Quickly, the residential blocks gave way to open fields and farmland.

"Where are you taking me?" Abby asked.

Hettie Mae pointed ahead. "There."

Abby recognized their destination as the building that housed the professional-training nonprofit that Bert had mentioned the other night. "Is that where I'll be doing the kitchen management class? You know, the one you all maneuvered me into?"

"That's right."

They swooped lower and circled the building twice before finally settling down in front.

Hettie Mae let go of Abby's arm. "How are you feeling? No motion sickness, I hope?"

"Actually, I've never flown in a dream before, at least not that I can remember. It felt wonderful."

"Knew you'd like it." She marched to the building's front door and pulled it open. "After you."

Once inside, Abby found herself following Hettie Mae down a long hallway to a classroom door. The door had a small window at eye level.

"Go ahead and take a peek," Hettie Mae said. "They can't see you."

Abby stepped closer and gasped again. Inside, she saw *herself* teaching a class! A dozen students, a mix of teenagers and adults, were listening attentively to what she — herself, oh dear, this was a tad confusing — was saying.

"Is this the future?" Abby asked.

"Perhaps. If you pay attention."

Abby turned to her friend. "What do you mean, *if*? What am I supposed to pay attention to?"

"Not me, that's for sure."

"I don't understand what's going on here."

"You don't need to. But you need to pay attention."

"To what?"

"To what happens next."

Abby shook her head, getting exasperated.

"Stop looking at me," Hettie Mae said firmly. "The next moment is key. Watch and you'll see."

Reluctantly, Abby returned her attention to the classroom.

A student raised his hand. He was in his mid-twenties, tall and lanky, with ebony skin and handsome features, dressed in work boots, blue jeans, and a red flannel shirt. Though Abby couldn't say why, she somehow knew that this young man used his hands for a living. Construction of some sort, she bet.

His manner was hesitant, as if he were unsure of the question he wanted to ask, or perhaps of his right to ask it.

Abby — or the version of herself inside the classroom — noticed his raised hand and gave him a nod. Through the closed door, she couldn't hear what either of them said, but as she watched his face, she felt a warm glow. The uncertainty in his brow seemed to ease. He liked her answer. Whatever she'd said had reassured him.

"You've always been an excellent teacher," Hettie Mae said. "Chocolate-making and teaching — two of your most impressive skills."

"Is this why I'm here? So I'll be encouraged to teach more?"

"Pay attention, dear."

Abby turned back toward the classroom and gasped yet again. The classroom was gone. Through the window, a swirling mist parted to reveal her own little kitchen at the chocolate shop, where the same young man was skillfully tempering chocolate. Her attention sharpened as she admired his technique. There was precision there — the result of practice, concentration, and enthusiasm. Even without knowing which chocolates he was making, she knew they'd be delicious.

"Hettie Mae," she said, "are you saying this young man will take the class and I'll hire him to help me at the shop?"

"Abby, dear," her friend said patiently, "stop looking at me. Keep your eye on the window."

With a sigh of frustration, Abby turned back to the window and found that her little kitchen was gone. The same young man was in a chef's uniform in a bustling kitchen, where he was plating a lovely filet mignon topped with asparagus spears over a bed of mashed sweet potatoes. He carried the plate through swinging kitchen doors into a beautiful restaurant. As Abby trailed behind him, she glanced at a wall and spied a framed newspaper story with his beaming face in a photo underneath a headline that read, "Tucker Johnson's brilliant take on Caribbean cuisine."

"Is this for real?" Abby asked. "Am I witnessing his future?"

"You might be," Hettie Mae said.

Through the window, the scene blurred again. Events seemed to speed up. From her seat in a pew, she saw the young man standing before a minister next to a young woman whose face Abby couldn't quite catch but who, she sensed, was someone she already knew. The mist swirled again and children rushed into the picture, dashing to and fro, jumping enthusiastically into the arms of the young man, whose hair now held a hint of gray. The scene shifted again, to a gathering of friends and family — a celebration — beneath a banner on the wall that proudly proclaimed, "Happy 50th Anniversary!" The young man — no longer young, his hair fully gray, his eyes still full of life — led his wife in a slow dance as the crowd cheered them on.

And seated at a table next to the dance floor, thinner than she was now, her hair completely white, her skin wrinkled with age, her eyes shining with joyful tears, watching her very dear friends dance, was a very old version of —

Herself?

"It won't happen like this," Hettie Mae said. "At least not exactly."

Abby could barely speak. "Is that really me there in the crowd, fifty years from now?"

"Fifty-four years, but who's counting?"

"But that would make me —"

"Positively ancient, but still around and enjoying life. You have a cane somewhere, I think."

Abby's mouth opened, but no words came out.

"No guarantees, of course," Hettie Mae said. "That's not how this works."

"Hettie Mae, I —"

Her friend cut her off. "Sorry, dear. Hate to be rude, but I'm out of time."

"Please don't go yet," Abby begged her. "You have to explain this."

"That's the one thing I can't do," Hettie Mae said regretfully. "You need to figure this out yourself."

Abby looked at her friend helplessly. "I don't even know where to start."

"You will." Her friend started to shimmer and fade. "When the moment happens, you'll feel it. Just remember this: Small gestures can make a world of difference. Acts of consideration and kindness are more powerful than you will ever know."

"Hettie Mae, wait —"

"You can do it, dear. I know it."

And with that, her friend was gone —

And Abby found herself jolting awake, once again clutching her comforter and wondering what this vivid, perplexing dream of hers might mean.

CHAPTER 11

The confounding thing about dreams, Abby told herself as the early morning light gradually crossed her bedroom and her heart rate settled back to normal, was that they didn't mean anything. She needed to be honest with herself about that. No, more than that, she needed to be very specific with herself and get over the ridiculous conceit that her dreams, vivid though they were, had some kind of special significance. Who was she kidding? Dreams were just dreams. The only thing going on here was her subconscious doing its usual problem-solving thing.

Yes, that had to be what was going on here — her subconscious chewing on something. It did that all the time. All she had to do was give it the space it needed to figure out what it needed to figure out. When it was ready, it would tell her. Most likely, what it was figuring out was something simple and prosaic, even boring. Maybe she'd forgotten something she needed to do. Maybe her subconscious was telling her to cut back on the late-night snacking. Or get a different pillow. Or or or….

For the next few moments, motionless in bed, she tried to encourage herself to think of other things instead. She had a busy day ahead of her — a bit of mental planning would be helpful. Or, she realized, she could think of more pleasurable topics … like John, for instance. A smile came to her lips. She'd enjoyed her lesson with him, far more than she'd expected. If she was reading things right, he'd enjoyed himself as well. It had been a long time — years, really — since she'd found herself spending time with a man she liked this way.

Yes, she admitted to herself. She felt an attraction toward him.

She swallowed back the surge of emotion that accompanied this acknowledgment. It was good — necessary, in fact — to be clear-headed and upfront about this. Because the reality was that, regardless of how she might feel, nothing was going to happen. She needed to understand and accept that. John was a widower with young children. Dating most likely wasn't a priority for him.

The sooner she moved past whatever she might be feeling and accepted that dating was out of the question, the better for both of them. They could be friends. Yes, being friends with John sounded perfect.

Without even looking, she knew her alarm clock was about to announce the start of the day. As always, she had a place to be and tasks to complete. She swung herself upright, hit the off button on her clock, showered, dressed, and made her way to the shop for yet another early session of chocolate-making.

The morning proved fruitful — amazing what a dose of clarity could do for one's productivity — and it was only as she finished her fourth batch of salted caramels and set them in the cooling tray that she realized something was still bugging her. The some-thing wasn't her vivid dream, nor her unrealistic imaginings about John.

No, it was something else, nagging softly at the edge of her awareness.

She caught a hint, like a faint whisper:

Something undone or unsettled. Something she could address right away, if she chose to.

A sigh escaped her lips. The state her life was in right now, was there anything that wasn't undone or unsettled? The shop was opening at eleven — barely fifteen minutes away. Her kitchen was a mess, and she needed to get it cleaned before heading up front.

But wait, she remembered. Today she had help coming in. Which meant —

Her thoughts were interrupted by the sound of

the front door opening and a familiar voice calling out, "Abby, it's me!"

The first big smile of the day made its way to her face. "Good morning, Anna!"

A few seconds later, James's daughter Anna popped through the kitchen's swinging doors. A cheerful twenty-one-year-old with a round face, big glasses, and a mass of wavy brown hair that seemed to sprout untamed from her head, Anna was decked out today in jeans, black boots, and a festive red-and-white sweater.

"How's everything this morning?" Anna asked, her gaze immediately taking in the kitchen's messy state.

"I'm so glad you're here today," Abby replied fervently. "This time of year…."

"I'm the one who's glad. What would starving students like me do without friendly shopkeepers like you offering us part-time work to help cover our tuition?"

Abby grinned. Anna was more than just a starving student — she was an exceptional one, a true scholar in the making. Now in her final year of college in Boston, she was busily applying for Ph.D. programs in American history, with a focus on the history of New England. In preparation for her future dissertation, she'd been coming home frequently throughout the fall to dig into the musty old archives in the basement of the town hall, seeking to shine a fresh light on Heartsprings Valley's rich past.

"You need help back here?" Anna asked.

"Oh, no, I'm good," Abby assured her.

"I'll get everything ready up front."

"Thank you." Abby sped through her cleanup tasks, the choreography almost instinctive after all these years, managing to finish seconds before the front bell rang to announce the arrival of the day's first customer.

Usually, when someone was helping in the front room, Abby would spend more time in the kitchen, making more chocolates to keep up with the seemingly endless demand. Yet today, for reasons she couldn't put her finger on, she hadn't followed that path. Instead, she'd cleaned up.

Why had she done that? Was it because of the undone, unsettled *something* bugging her?

Almost without realizing what she was doing, she reached for her phone and called Bert. "Quick question," she said when he picked up. "What's the name of the person who runs the training nonprofit?"

"Carla Holcombe," Bert replied. "I told her you agreed to teach the course, by the way. You're still on board, right?"

"Yes, totally. I have a few spare moments, so I thought I'd give her a call."

"I'll text you the number."

"Thanks!"

A few seconds later, the number arrived and Abby found herself dialing.

A woman picked up after two rings. "Heartsprings Valley Training Center, Carla speaking. How may I help you today?"

"Hi, Carla, we haven't met yet. My name is Abby Donovan. Bert Winters may have mentioned me?"

"Oh, my — yes, he did," Carla said, her voice filling with enthusiasm. "Thank you so much for agreeing to teach our introductory kitchen management course. And thank you for calling. I can't wait to meet you in person. Bert mentioned how busy your store is right now. I was planning to drop by and introduce myself."

"You're welcome to drop by anytime." Then she surprised herself by adding, "But I'm wondering, any chance I could swing by the center right now? I've driven past a thousand times but never been inside, and for the next couple of hours I have help here at the store, so I was thinking, if it's okay with you, maybe I could come to you?"

"That would be wonderful," Carla said. "I'm here right now."

"See you in thirty?"

"Thirty it is."

As she shrugged into her coat, Abby's gut confirmed that going to the training center was a good thing. Her dream — and her sense of something undone — were probably about the class she'd agreed to teach. Visiting the training center would help her prepare. She could check out the classroom and hear directly from Carla what the center was hoping for.

"Anna," she said as she stepped into the front room, "I have a few errands." She grabbed a box of chocolates from the wall shelf and slipped it into her handbag. "I'll be back in ninety minutes. Anything you need from me before I head out?"

"All good here," Anna said from her spot behind the counter. "See you soon!"

With her car at home just a few short blocks away, it wasn't long before Abby was heading down the valley's main road toward the training center. As she passed a farmhouse, she smiled at the sight of the owners stringing holiday lights on the front porch while their three kids and a frisky dog busied themselves building a snowman in the front yard. There wasn't a lot of snow on the ground yet, but enough had fallen for the kids to have no trouble fashioning a round torso and head for their frosty friend. Yes, she thought with a smile, winter had definitely arrived.

As her destination neared, Abby tried to recall what she knew about the training center. The answer was — not much. It had moved into its current location a few years back. Aside from that, she was drawing a blank.

Fortunately, her lack of knowledge was about to change. She pulled into the center's gravel lot and parked near the front door. As she got out, her boots crunching on the gravel, she felt a shiver of recognition: She'd been here before, in almost this very spot, though only in her dream.

Shaking off the thought with annoyance — dreams were just dreams — she made her way into the building. She found herself in a long hallway with doors at regular intervals. A quick glance through a small window in one of the doors — once again, just like her dream — confirmed that the doors led to classrooms.

She'd probably been here before and forgotten, she told herself. Or seen a photo and forgotten. There were a million logical explanations. The idea that a dream could —

From the end of the hallway, she heard a voice say, "Hello, can I help you?"

Abby turned. A woman was bustling toward her. She had short brown hair and a pleasant face, and was dressed in sneakers, jeans, and a leather bomber jacket. As she got closer, Abby saw flecks of grey in her hair and realized the woman was probably in her mid-forties, like her.

"Hi," Abby said, "are you Carla?"

"You must be Abby," Carla replied warmly. She reached out and took hold of Abby's hand. "So pleased to meet you. Thank you so much for coming out here this morning."

"Please to meet you, too." The woman's warmth

was palpable, her face alive with enthusiasm. Abby was suddenly very glad she'd been maneuvered by Bert into teaching here. "I almost hate to admit this, but I've never actually been inside the center."

"Then let me give you a tour." With that, Carla took her by the arm and led her down the hall. "It won't take but a minute — what you see is what you get. We have twelve classrooms here, including one with a kitchen — that's where you'll be — and one with a workshop for woodworking. My job — I'm executive director — is to keep the classrooms busy and funded."

"How long have you been here?"

"We moved into this space a few years ago, but my husband and I started the center twelve years ago in Eagle Cove. When this space became available, we got a bargain on the rent and knew we had to snap it up."

Carla opened a classroom door to let Abby peek inside. A quick glance revealed a typical classroom, with chairs and tables facing a big chalkboard along one wall. "What kind of courses do you offer?"

"Adult education, with a focus on job-related skills."

"And that means…."

"Everything from getting your GED to learning how to use computers to learning how to fix a sink," Carla said as they made their way back into the hall. "The key for us is what's practical and useful in today's job market. Let's go to the culinary classroom."

At the far end of the long hall, Carla held a door open and stepped aside. "What do you think?"

Very quickly, Abby realized she liked what she saw. There were nine separate prep islands, each with a sink, two burners, and a generous stainless steel countertop, all facing a big chalkboard wall. Against the side walls were rows of ovens and refrigerators and dishwashers, along with closed cabinets for dishes and utensils. The far end of the room had nice big windows facing the back of the building. Bright midday sun streamed in. The overall effect was clean, fresh, and up-to-date.

"This looks terrific," Abby told Carla. "I'm impressed. Was the space updated recently?"

"Before we moved in, by a company that ran cooking classes here."

"Whoever set this up did a very nice job."

"Agreed." Anxiety flitted across Carla's face. "Will the space be all right for you, do you think?"

"For the class, you mean?" Abby replied. "Oh, I imagine so. Could we perhaps talk about what kind of focus you're after?"

"Of course," Carla said. "Let's head to the office."

CHAPTER 12

*a*bby followed Carla into a classroom two doors down that had been subdivided into a meeting room and a small private office.

At that moment, they heard a loud bump through the wall.

"That's the electrician," Carla said. "Nothing to worry about. We're putting in new A/V cabling." She ushered Abby into the office and gestured to a chair in front of the desk. "It's usually busier around here, but the fall classes wrapped last week and the winter session doesn't start till January. We schedule it this way to avoid the holiday crush."

The holidays are a busy time for everyone," Abby said as she settled into the chair.

"We try to use this time to finish our prep for the coming year." she said, then added wryly, "but mostly we end up playing catchup on everything we've been putting off."

Abby chuckled. "I know the feeling, though my slack time starts after Valentine's Day."

Carla smiled. "I've heard great things about your chocolates. I can't believe I haven't tried them yet."

Abby reached into her handbag and pulled out the box she'd brought with her. "For you. Think of it as an early Christmas gift."

"Oh," Carla said, her eyes lighting up. "Thank so you much! You didn't have to."

"I wanted to."

Carla gestured toward the lid. "Is it okay if I...?"

"Please."

Eagerly, Carla slipped the red ribbon off the box and lifted the lid to reveal eighteen assorted chocolates. "Oh, my," she whispered. "These are beautiful." She leaned closer and breathed in. "And they smell wonderful."

"I hope you like them."

"I'm going to savor these, each and every one. Though you've now presented me with an ethical dilemma."

"Oh?" Abby said, her eyebrows rising.

Carla's eyes were twinkling. "Do I share them with my husband — or keep them all for myself?"

They both laughed.

Abby said, "That's one conundrum you'll have to figure out on your own."

For the next few minutes, the two of them talked about the class and the students the class was likely to attract. "The intent is introductory," Carla said. "Kind of a 'dip-your-toes-before-diving-in' thing."

"Most of the students will be new to the field?"

"That's what we've seen when we've run the class in the past."

"Okay," Abby said, chewing her lips as she absorbed what she was hearing. "Would it be okay if I give this some thought? Maybe we could meet again next week to discuss more?"

Carla nodded in agreement. "I'd love to swing by your shop, if that's okay with you."

"That sounds great."

"There is one thing I'm hoping we can finalize now."

"What's that?"

"The course name." She swung her computer screen around to let Abby see it. "I'm finishing the brochure and flyer so I can get them printed and distributed. The name of your class is the final piece of the puzzle."

Abby considered. "The suggestion I heard from Bert — 'Introduction to Professional Kitchen Management' — works for me."

"Perfect," Carla said, typing in the words. She hit a button on her computer and behind her, a printer started whirring away. "I'm printing you a copy."

"Thanks," Abby said, rising to her feet. "I should probably get going. Lots to do."

Carla grabbed the flyer from the printer and handed it to her, then paused. "Actually, could I ask a favor? On your way out, could you pin a copy of this on the bulletin board up near the front entrance? There's a spot on the left side for it."

"Of course," Abby replied.

Carla printed a second copy, handed it to her, then made her way around the desk. "It was so great meeting you today."

"A pleasure meeting you, too."

Carla's eyes were filled with warmth. "Thank you again for agreeing to help us. Talk with you soon!"

As Abby strode down the hall, she felt lighter, as if a burden — an undone task — had been lifted from her shoulders. At the bulletin board, she plucked two unused tacks from the board, located the spot on the left side of the board for the flyer, and pinned it up.

Behind her, she became aware she had an audience. She turned and found she'd been joined by a nice-looking young man in his mid-twenties, tall and lanky, with ebony skin and shy brown eyes, carrying a toolbox and a long loop of cabling over his shoulder.

Abby recalled what Carla had said about the A/V cabling being upgraded, and she gave the young man a smile.

The man smiled in return, then shifted his attention to the flyer she'd just posted. Though his demeanor was hesitant, his curiosity was evident when he said, "Excuse me, ma'am. Is that the list of classes starting in January?"

"It is," she said.

He stepped closer to read the list. As he did so, Abby caught his profile and a jolt of recognition surged through her. This was the young man from her dream!

Even as the realization raced through her, another part of her immediately pushed back. The idea that her dream was anything but a dream was nonsense. And for it to be a premonition — utterly ridiculous.

Yet how else to explain what was happening in this very moment?

"Is there a particular class you're interested in?" she found herself asking.

"The one on kitchen management," the young man said. "I'm wondering about that one."

"Well," Abby said, collecting her thoughts. "The goal is to provide an introduction to the field. It's a big field, as you may know, and a challenging one. We'll be touching on a number of important topics, including menu planning, inventory management, personnel training, cost control, and more."

He was nodding intently. "It's a field I want to learn more about."

"You want to see if you might be a good fit."

"That's right."

"Is food a passion of yours?"

"Oh, yeah," he said, his eyes lighting up. "Ever since I was a kid. Like, I look at a dish or take a bite of something and I'm thinking, 'How did they make that?'"

Abby smiled. "Sounds like there are cooking traditions in your family that you've tried your hand at?"

The young man's expression faded. "Not really, no." After a pause, he added, "I grew up in the foster system. The people I lived with weren't into cooking."

"Oh," Abby said, not sure how to respond.

"Sorry," he said immediately, aware of her uncertainty. "Didn't mean to open with that. I usually hold off before going there. It's just…." He seemed puzzled. "I guess I felt comfortable telling you."

"Well, I'm glad you did," she replied, realizing the truth of her words as she spoke them.

"The important thing is," he continued, "I made it through. I got lucky — I stayed in the same place the last three years of high school and had a great teacher who watched out for me and made sure I graduated. After high school, I joined the Army, saw the world, got training in electronics. But now…."

"Now you're wondering if you'd like to try a different field."

His eyes flashed affirmation. "My training in the Army was great — I work as an electrician now. But fixing appliances and running cables isn't the same as cooking an amazing meal."

"Being an electrician isn't your passion."

"There's something, I don't know, *soulful* about good food. Somehow, it feels more important." He brought himself up short, as if embarrassed. "Sorry, that sounds crazy, doesn't it?"

"Not at all," she hastened to assure him. "What you feel about food is what every great cook and baker feels."

He seemed heartened by that. He extended his hand. "I'm Tucker."

Just like the dream. Trying not to show how startled she was, she took his hand in hers. "Abby."

"Pleased to meet you, Abby."

Pushing aside the coincidence, she said, "So, Tucker, when you dream of baking or cooking, what do you dream of?"

A small laugh escaped him. "Something delicious and beautiful. All kinds of stuff. I watch the cooking shows and I'm amazed at what folks can do. I like the idea of small dishes that pack a lot of punch — each bite full of great flavors."

"Do you find yourself gravitating more toward a certain kind of cuisine? Or desserts?"

He shrugged. "I don't know yet. I like all of it, maybe because I don't know enough yet. When I have time, I experiment with all kinds of things

— meats and vegetables and cakes and dishes with French names I can't even pronounce."

Abby grinned. She liked this young man. "French pretty much escapes me, too. It took me forever to learn how to say 'vichyssoise' correctly."

"Vichyssoise?" he repeated. "Which one is that?"

"It's the thick soup made of boiled and puréed potatoes, leeks, onions, chicken stock and cream, usually served cold."

"I think I saw that being made. Do you chop potatoes and leeks, cook them, simmer them in stock, then puree and let cool, then add the cream when you're ready to serve?"

"Your memory is excellent."

Anxiety flashed through his eyes. "When it comes to recipes, sure. But when it comes to learning about the other aspects of kitchen management...."

"Only one way to find out. That's what the January sessions are about. I'll be the instructor, by the way."

He seemed pleased to hear that. "Are you a chef?"

"A chocolatier. I run a small shop here in Heart-springs Valley."

"Abby's Chocolate Heaven?" he said, his face lighting up. "Across the square from the Heart-springs Valley Cafe?"

"That's the one."

"I've been there. I don't think you were there that

day. Your shop looks and smells amazing. The chocolates you make are incredible."

His praise was touching. He seemed so sincere.

"Tucker, will I see you in class in January?"

He swallowed as if pushing back emotion — like he was surprised and grateful to receive the encouragement. A big smile transformed his face. "Can't wait. I'm gonna go find Carla and sign up right now."

CHAPTER 13

*T*he glow Abby felt as she headed back to town easily banished the "unsettled" feeling that had been weighing her down all morning. The world seemed brighter somehow. More open to possibility. She still didn't understand her strange dream — the idea of it being predictive was, of course, beyond silly — but the ways in which the dream seemed to foreshadow what she'd seen and heard this morning couldn't be easily explained.

Then don't explain it, she ordered herself, her pragmatic side taking over. *Just let it be*. She allowed the idea to roll through her head and found herself nodding in agreement. Yes, pushing her dream questions to her mental back burner was exactly what she wanted to do.

The afternoon seemed to fly by, with customers flocking to the shop and keeping her and Anna hopping. Finally, as dusk settled in, the rush eased, Anna headed home, and Abby settled in behind the counter with a tired but contented sigh, preparing to open her laptop and catch up on her expenses. For the moment at least, the shop was quiet. In the background, the town's radio station was serenading her with a big-band version of "Jingle Bells."

As she hummed along, she heard the door open and glanced over to see John closing the shop door behind him.

She tried to ignore the lift in her heart. "Good evening, John."

He approached with a big grin. "Evening! Have I mentioned before how great this place smells?"

She smiled, aware of how pleased she was to see him. "To what do I owe the pleasure?"

"I'm trying to get a head start on the party planning, and I'm hoping I can pick your brain about a few things."

"Of course."

"I've spoken separately with Melody and James, so I have a pretty good idea what each of them is after. That part is straightforward." He sighed and shook his head. "But for the life of me, I don't see how this double-surprise is going to get pulled off."

"It does pose a challenge," she agreed.

"They want to invite a lot of the same guests and place orders with a lot of the same shops. My concern is that, without meaning to, someone's gonna spill the beans."

"Who are the orders with?"

"Here's the list." He pulled a piece of paper out of his coat pocket and unfolded it. "They both want scones and other treats from Holly at the Heartsprings Valley Cafe. Melody wants hot spiced cider from Northland Orchard, and James wants cider from an orchard farmer named" — he squinted at his list — "Gabe."

"Gabe runs Northland Orchard. It's just outside of town."

"Ah," he said, "that helps."

"Who else is on the list?"

"You are," he said, shooting her a grin.

Abby smiled. "James ordered a chocolate cake, and Melody wants chocolates."

Together, they read through the list. "The good news," she said, "is there's a lot of overlap. What about the guests?"

He nodded and handed her a second sheet of paper. "There's overlap here, too."

"Which makes sense," she said as she scanned the names. "This is shaping up to be quite an event."

"You're telling me. I'd forgotten how much planning a party takes. It's been a while since I put one on. Not since —"

Abruptly, he stopped talking. Abby looked up

from the guest list and saw a shadow passing over his face.

"Listen," she said, guessing where his head was. "You don't have to do this alone. Like I said last night, I'm happy to help."

"You sure?" Once again, she sensed that he felt obligated to ask but was really hoping she would say —

"Of course. Happy to." Briskly, she added, "How about this? I'll call the folks doing the orders and let them know the deal. They'll all keep their lips zipped, I promise."

"Thank you."

"And you can focus on the guests." Her brow furrowed as she returned to the names. "Some of these people are, um, how do I put it…."

"Gossips?" John asked teasingly.

"Talkative," Abby replied with a smile. "It's probably best to be completely frank and above-board with everyone about the whole deal, because folks are going to figure it out anyway."

"Got it."

"Ask them not to spill the beans to James or Melody."

"Got it."

"You know," she said as she considered the planning and how it might all play out, "this double-surprise might actually happen."

"We make a great team," he said, his gaze intensifying.

She blinked and turned away, her cheeks flushing with unwanted emotion.

"So," she said, desperate for a safe topic, "any questions come up after our caramel-making session last night?"

He considered her question. "Not really. I learned a ton. You made everything seem very doable, and also fun. You're a terrific teacher."

"Thank you," she said, feeling both pleased and self-conscious about his assessment.

"I'd like to be sure I have a good handle on the caramels. Would it be okay if we make them again at our next lesson, and also include them in the session with the kids?"

"Practice makes perfect?"

"That's the idea."

"Of course."

"Great." He paused, as if aware that his stated excuse for swinging by — party advice — had already been dealt with. "I guess I should get going."

"Feel free to come by anytime," Abby said, hoping she was coming across as friendly and encouraging and *normal*.

"I'll do that," he said, his eyes flashing. "See you soon."

CHAPTER 14

*I*n the days that followed, Abby ended up seeing quite a lot of John. Party planning was never as straightforward as one hoped, of course; inevitably, questions arose. But John seemed to run into an inordinate number of issues, and all of them, it seemed, required Abby's guidance.

Was it wrong that, as his visits became a regular part of her day, she found herself anticipating the moment he walked into her little shop? Was it silly that, when he gazed at her with such warmth and interest, her heart gave a little flutter? Was it crazy to wonder whether maybe, just maybe, his interest in her extended beyond party planning and chocolate lessons?

On the Wednesday evening of their second private lesson, she heard the shop bell ring, right on time, followed by the sound of John's voice. "Abby, it's me."

"Back here," she called out from the kitchen as she gave the marble countertop a careful wipe-down.

He pushed through the swinging doors, a big grin on his face, and gestured to the back. "Same as last week? Coat on the…."

"Yes." She gave the countertop a final wipe as he eased by her. "What's the latest on the planning?"

"Forty confirmed guests and counting. I'm betting we end up around fifty." Coat hung, he made his way to the sink to wash his hands. "Everyone's excited about being in on the surprise."

"Surprises are fun."

"I talked with a bunch of folks for the first time this week. People whose names I'd heard but didn't know yet." Rinsing done, he dried his hands and turned to her expectantly. "So what's the plan for tonight's lesson?"

"You asked to make the caramels again. Is that still what you'd like?"

"Yep."

"All right," she said with a smile. "You know what to do. Get to work."

He blinked. "Just like that — dive right in?"

"Practice makes perfect."

It took him a few seconds to get oriented, but quickly enough, he found the double boiler, added two inches of water, and set it on the burner. "Choco-late in the fridge?"

"That's right."

She watched him grab the chocolate blocks from the fridge, set them on a chopping board, and pick up a knife. With a confidence that came from knowing what he needed to do, he set about cutting the chocolate into half-inch chunks.

"Mind if I ask a personal question?" he said as he chopped away.

"Sure," she replied cautiously.

"You opened the shop eight years ago, after you moved here — and after your divorce?"

Abby felt her stomach tighten. "That's right. The marriage ended eight years ago. I opened the shop shortly after signing my divorce papers."

He glanced at her sympathetically. "I'm sorry. That must have been very painful."

She weighed her response before replying. His question was indeed personal; she didn't normally share details with people she didn't trust. But as she gazed into John's kind eyes, she sensed he wasn't asking to pry or because nosiness was part of his nature. Quite the opposite: He struck her as someone who valued discretion. When she'd asked him about his architectural work, he hadn't bragged about his famous client, though he easily could have. In fact, the only information he'd shared about Melody and

James was a compliment about James's talent as a furniture craftsman.

Yes, she decided, she was okay sharing the truth with him. "It was painful," she said with a sigh. "We grew apart. We both had busy jobs. I was an accountant in a big firm, putting in long hours for my clients. He was in sales and traveled a lot. I wanted to start a family, and he wanted to wait. I wanted to launch a small business — chocolate-making has been a passion of mine since I was a kid — and he wanted me to stick with the security of a full-time job with the accounting firm. And then he met someone."

His mouth tightened. "I'm sorry."

"I was sorry, too. About all of it." Somewhat to her surprise, she added, "The end of my marriage — it really hurt. I was angry and disappointed with him, of course, but I was also upset with myself. I agonized over everything that had happened, trying to understand what I'd done wrong. It took me a long time — years, really — to figure out what had been in front of me all along, staring me in the face."

His eyes hadn't left hers. "Namely?"

She exhaled. "He and I weren't the right fit. We started dating in college. We were in the same social circle — my friends were going out with his friends. As we got to know each other, we found we liked each other well enough, and we fell into dating."

"You weren't in love?"

She shook her head. "I realize now that we became a couple because it was easy and expected. He and I liked each other, my friends and family liked him, his friends and family liked me, so I thought, 'Yes, this is what love is about.' Even after I realized that what we had wasn't what other couples had, I didn't give up. I did everything I could to make our marriage work." She ignored the pang of disappointment that still, after all these years, hadn't gone away. "If I'm being honest about how everything happened, he tried to make it work, too, at least up to a certain point. I like to think there were times we came close. But in the end…."

"Are you two still in touch?"

She shook her head. "He remarried about a year after the divorce, got a big promotion, and moved to Seattle."

She realized the water on the stove was boiling. "Behind you," she said.

He turned and shut off the burner. "Two thirds of the chocolate, right?"

"That's right."

Quickly, he divided the chocolate chunks into three piles, added two piles to the top pot, and set the pot with the chocolate on top of the pot of simmering water.

"So that's when you moved here and opened this

place," he said as he grabbed a spatula and thermometer from the counter.

"That's right."

"You committed yourself to making your shop a success."

She nodded. "A long road. A lot of work."

"Worth it?" he asked, giving the chocolate a good stir.

"Definitely. No regrets. I took a big risk leaving the accounting firm, but fortunately it worked out."

"I joined a big architecture firm right out of school," he said. "Worked there for years before starting out on my own."

"What led you to make the leap?"

He paused his stirring, then said quietly, "After we lost Diane, I realized there are no guarantees. There's only now."

He hadn't mentioned his wife until now — she'd been waiting for him to do so. Perhaps this was a signal that he was ready to share more about that sad and painful topic?

"I'm very sorry about your wife," she said quietly. "I heard you lost her three years ago."

He nodded. "Ovarian cancer. After her diagnosis, we had her for four years. She died a few days after the twins' seventh birthday. I think she decided to hang on long enough to watch them blow out the candles on their cake."

"I'm so sorry," she said.

He swallowed, his eyes suddenly bright with moisture.

Immediately, Abby grabbed a fresh paper towel and handed it to him.

"Sorry," he said, setting the spatula down. "It's still hard to talk about. I expect it always will be."

"You have nothing to apologize for. I can only imagine how incredibly difficult this has been for you and Maggie and Jacob."

He blew his nose. "Very hard. But in the past year, we've started doing better. Moving to Heartsprings Valley is a big part of why. Having Mom and Dad close by has really helped."

Abby grabbed the spatula and gave the chocolate a good stir while he collected himself and cleaned up. As he rinsed his hands again in the sink, he glanced over at her.

"I take it your parents aren't nearby?"

"I lost my dad six years ago and my mom four years ago," Abby said softly. "Heart attacks both."

"I'm so sorry."

"I am, too," she said, pushing the rush of emotion away. "I miss them every day."

"You were close?"

"Mom and I shared a love of baking and chocolate-making, and Dad was my biggest cheerleader."

His gaze was sympathetic. "Any siblings in the picture?"

She shook her head. "Only child. I have cousins

on the West Coast, but we don't see each other as often as we'd like."

"So Heartsprings Valley is home for you now."

"It is," she said, suddenly aware of how glad that made her feel. "Despite the disappointments I've had in my life, despite the losses, I know how much I have to be grateful for. I live in a beautiful town. I'm blessed with wonderful friends. Every day, I get to work at the small business I built from scratch with my own hands, making products I'm proud of."

"Work can be a lifesaver," he said. "It has been for me."

"I agree. It forces you to focus on something other than…."

"Other than what we've lost." He dipped the thermometer into the melted chocolate, nodding at the temperature, then added the remaining chocolate chunks. "It took me a while to understand that. When I returned to the office after the funeral, I was pretty useless. Gradually, I became less useless. I had colleagues depending on me, deadlines to hit, specs to finish, city planners to meet — all of which required my energy and focus." He picked up the spatula and gave the chocolate a stir. "Though after a while, I realized the work itself wasn't going to be enough."

"Not enough for …?"

"For me. To keep me fully engaged and committed."

"What did you need for that?"

"A change."

Abby's heart rate quickened. *She needed a change, too.* "You weren't happy at the firm?"

He shrugged. "I wasn't unhappy, but I also wasn't fulfilled. I had good colleagues, and some of the projects were interesting and rewarding. But the firm does large-scale commercial and municipal development — skyscrapers, transit terminals, that kind of thing — and I wanted projects that were more intimate and personal."

"Projects like homes?"

He nodded. "There's a saying in architecture: 'Make no small plans.' But I don't agree with that approach. The homes, offices, and workshops I work on are important. We live most of our lives in these spaces. They matter. We shouldn't talk about them in ways that diminish them."

He checked the chocolate's temperature, nodding when he saw it where he wanted it, then lifted the pot from the burner and set it on a towel on the counter to cool. "You mentioned last week that your kitchen is too...."

"Too tight. The space works for one person, but barely."

"Do you see yourself expanding the business someday?"

She felt her chest tighten. There was that word again — *expanding.* "I'd like to, yes."

"But you feel yourself constrained by...?"

"Lack of space. Lack of time. Every available moment, I'm here in this kitchen, making chocolates."

"So if you had more space...."

"I'd hire help."

"Which would free you up to...."

"Launch a new line of chocolates," she heard herself saying.

"You mentioned that during our first lesson," he said, his brow furrowing. "What does that involve?"

Abby took a deep breath, surprised but pleased to be sharing this. "It's really all about the chocolates themselves. The ones I sell up front are my crowd-pleasers. I pay close attention to what my customers enjoy most and do my best to give them what they want."

"But your new line is...?"

"More to my personal taste. I love my crowd-pleasers, don't get me wrong, but my preference is for chocolates with more cocoa."

"Darker chocolates."

"That's right. I also like experimenting with ingredients you don't normally associate with chocolates."

"Give me an example."

"Well," she said, considering. "The piece you picked for your afternoon hike — the one with coffee and cardamom — is actually the first chocolate in the new line."

"How did you land on that combination of ingredients, by the way?"

"Experimenting, plain and simple. I was surprised, too."

"Okay," he said, nodding. "So your idea is to come up with other chocolates that also have that 'eat-me-slowly-and-linger-over-how-amazing-they-taste' kind of experience?"

'I'm experimenting on one now with candied ginger."

"Ginger? I don't really associate that with chocolate. Sounds pretty far out of the mainstream."

"Folks with expert knowledge are likely to be familiar with it, but others…."

"You're aiming for a niche or specialty market."

"That's my expectation."

"You'll sell most of them online?"

"That's the idea."

"And the marketing?"

"A few ideas, but haven't fleshed out a plan yet. One thing I know I'll do is enter the chocolates in competitions."

"Well," he said with a grin, "if you need a taste-tester…."

"You'll be my guinea pig?"

"Gladly."

His gaze was unwavering. For once, Abby didn't shy away. He was so easy to talk with. Truly, he had a gift for listening and making her feel comfortable.

His brown eyes had a lighter color in them, she realized.

"Your eyes have a hint of green," she said without thinking.

He blinked, taken aback by the shift in topic. "That's right."

She felt her cheeks flush pink. *What was she doing?* "Sorry, I didn't mean to say that."

"It's fine," he said. "I mean, it's true. My eyes are brown with a sliver of green. I'm told they become greener when I'm emotional."

"What are you emotional about right now?"

He was about to reply but instead brought himself up short, as if surprised. A flush appeared on his cheeks. "Being here," he finally said, green flashing. "Learning how to make chocolates from a great teacher."

Warmth spread through her. "Thank you," she managed to say.

As if aware of the awkwardness of the moment and eager to move to safer ground, he gestured toward the drafty window.

"Have you considered moving the shop to a different space?"

"Not really, no. I bought this place a few years ago after the previous owner moved away."

"So you're committed to the location and want to expand your business, but constrained by lack of space and lack of time." He pointed to the back door. "Do you mind if I…?"

She nodded, unsure what he was referring to. He made his way to the back door and stepped outside into the backyard. She followed, watching from the doorway as he examined the rear of the building and then knelt down to inspect the foundation closely. The night air was sharp, the cold seeping through her sweater.

"You could expand back here," he said.

"It would be a lot of work," she replied immediately.

"Some, but maybe not as much as you think." He looked again at the roof, his mind clearly off and running. "Extending the foundation, reshingling, shifting the drain spouts, updated gas and electrical, a new vent stack…."

It was fascinating to watch him envision a kitchen extension out of nothing. So powerful was his quiet confidence that she felt herself being carried along, somehow able to see it as well.

"More countertop space," she said. "An island large enough for three people to temper at once."

"What else?"

"Another refrigerator. A new sink. Bigger and deeper."

He shot her a knowing look. "A second dishwasher?"

A gasp escaped her. "Yes!"

He laughed. "Everyone says yes to that, by the way."

She joined him in laughing. "Who wouldn't?"

"In all seriousness," he said, "I'd be happy to work with you on ideas when you're ready. You deserve a space that allows you to expand and grow."

CHAPTER 15

*J*ohn was a fast learner, it turned out. Not only had he remembered the next steps in the salted caramel recipe, he completed them with skill. His tempering technique in particular was quite good. Some of her students had a natural feel for that critical step, while others struggled. John was one of the former, his movements sure and confident. After pouring the warm chocolate onto the cool marble countertop, he used a scraper to spread the chocolate and work it back together, coaxing it with skill to the desired thickness and finish, pausing only to measure its temperature.

"It's kind of like spreading plaster on walls," he said at one point.

He was probably right about that, Abby realized, though she didn't have enough experience with home renovation to know for sure.

Regardless, the salted caramels that he made were excellent — fully up to her exacting standards.

"Think I'm ready for the big test?" he asked as he helped her clean up.

"You mean the lesson with the kids on Saturday? Absolutely."

He grinned. "I can't wait. Should be a lot of fun."

"Have Maggie and Jacob settled on the chocolate they want to make?"

"The debate is raging. Maggie's been studying your brochure like it's a map to buried treasure. Three, four, five times a day, she announces a new choice."

Abby laughed. "And Jacob?"

"He already knows what he wants. He liked the piece he picked for the hike, so he wants us to learn to make those so we can have more whenever he wants."

"Very practical-minded of him. What's Maggie's take on that?"

"She's not ready to agree, but she really liked that piece as well, so I suspect she'll eventually land in the same place."

Three days later, John's prediction was proved right. The day dawned bright and clear. Abby got to the shop early and, between making fresh batches of chocolates, gathered up everything she needed for the afternoon class. When Anna arrived to manage the counter, Abby wrestled a box stuffed with supplies into her arms and carried it to the rec center, about a block off the town square and an easy walk from the shop. Two round trips later, she had everything she needed and was ready to go.

She took in the rec center's kitchen, trying to decide where to set up. It was a big space designed for catered events, with ovens and sinks and granite counters along the walls and four marble-topped prep islands in the center. Today's class included just John, Maggie, and Jacob, which meant only one of the islands would be needed.

As Abby immersed herself in getting everything set up and prepped, she lost track of time, the flow of her work effortless and satisfying. She loved what she did, and she loved sharing what she knew. She was still smiling when the cuckoo clock on the wall announced with a cheerful chirp that it was one o'clock. From the other side of the swinging doors, she heard the sound of children gabbing loudly and then —

John and the twins barreled in. The twins went quiet, eyes widening as they took in their surroundings.

"Good afternoon, Abby," John said with a grin.

"Good afternoon, John," she said with a smile. "Maggie and Jacob, it's great to see you again."

"Thank you, Ms. Donovan," the twins said in unison.

"Please, call me Abby."

"Abby," Maggie said, her gaze darting around the room, "this kitchen is *huge*."

Abby smiled. "It's a big one, isn't it? It's designed to support lunches and dinners here at the rec center. Catering crews have a lot to do during big events, so a space like this can make all the difference." She gestured to a coat rack near the door. "Hang up your coats, wash your hands, and join me here at the prep area."

The kids and John did as requested, then stood before her. Maggie was beaming with excitement, while Jacob seemed subdued and nonchalant but perhaps more interested than he was willing to let on.

"Maggie and Jacob and John, I'm so glad we're doing this today. We're going to have a lot of fun. You ready to get started?"

"I am *soooo* ready," Maggie said, barely able to contain herself.

Abby smiled. "How about you, Jacob?"

Jacob glanced at his sister and then at Abby, weighing his response. "I guess so," he finally said.

Abby gave him an encouraging nod, aware that his interest level was nowhere near his sister's. "First things first." From a grocery bag, she pulled out three crisp white aprons, two of them kid-size.

"For me?" Maggie gasped.

"For each of you. Yours to keep."

"Nice branding," John said as he slipped his on,

gesturing to the "Abby's Chocolate Heaven" logo on the front.

"This is awesome," Maggie said emphatically as she tied hers around her waist.

Jacob was frowning, clearly not as enthused. "Do I have to?"

"Think of it as a uniform, kiddo," John said. "And the kitchen is your playing field. Turn around and I'll tie you in."

With a resigned shrug, Jacob accepted the inevitable and complied.

"You three look great," Abby said. "With every new class, I begin by sharing four important points. First, we're here to have fun. During our afternoon together in this kitchen, I want us relaxed and enthusiastic, eager to dive into the wonderful world of chocolates, and prepared for a great time."

"I'm super-prepared and super-enthusiastic," Maggie said.

Abby laughed. "The second point is, we're here to learn. Very few people actually know how to make chocolates. By the time this class is over, you'll be among those select few."

Jacob perked up at that. Perhaps he hadn't considered the class from that angle and liked the idea of possessing specialized knowledge?

"Third, we're here to be safe. We'll be handling knives, using burners, and boiling liquids. There's a right way to do these things and many wrong ways

to do these things. I'll be showing you the right way."
She paused to let that sink in. "My expectation is that
you will make every effort to be careful. Do I have
your agreement on that?"

Solemnly, the kids nodded.

"Good," Abby said. "Which brings us to the
fourth point: Safety aside, mistakes are no big deal."

"You mean," Jacob said, "it's okay to mess up a
recipe?"

"Yes. It's completely okay."

The answer seemed to puzzle him. "Why's that?"

"Because mistakes are inevitable. Here in this
kitchen or in any kitchen, for that matter, it's simply
impossible to get everything right every time. I've
made countless mistakes myself. Every kind of goof
you can think of — the wrong ingredient, the wrong
amount, the wrong temperature, the wrong technique — you name it, I've muffed it. Every cook and
baker and chocolatier in the world will tell you the
same thing."

"Every single one?" Maggie said.

"Every single one. Kitchen disaster stories are
universal. I promise you that."

Jacob's eyes lit up. He leaned over and whispered
in Maggie's ear.

Maggie giggled. "Dad, tell Abby about
Thanksgiving."

John chuckled. "Abby doesn't want to hear about
that."

"Daaaaad," two voices said in unison.

He gave Abby a knowing smile, then shrugged. "I'm sure you two can tell it better."

And with that, the kids were off, treating Abby to a breathless and extremely detailed accounting of "The Great Thanksgiving Turkey Disaster." They told their tale with gusto, encouraged by Abby's "Oh, no!" and "No way!" and "Oh, dear!" at appropriate moments.

They really were adorable, the two of them. Their excitement was contagious. When they were in sync, as they were in that moment, they made a great team.

"Okay, time to focus," Abby finally said as the story wound down. "Have the two of you decided which chocolate you'd like to make today?"

The twins exchanged a glance before Maggie said, very soberly, "This was a very difficult decision to make."

"Not for me," Jacob said. "I knew right away."

Maggie shot him a sour look. "Did not."

"Did too."

"Only because it's the only chocolate you know."

"I know tons of chocolates."

"Do not."

"Do too."

"Name one chocolate Abby makes."

"The marshmallow one."

"Name a different one."

"Why should I?"

"Because if you don't, that proves you can't."

"No it doesn't."

"Kids," John said warningly.

Abby tried to keep a smile from her face. Bickering siblings were nothing new to her — dozens of families and kids had taken her classes over the years. This twosome, though a tad testy, still managed to make bickering thoroughly adorable.

"Maggie," she said, "tell me how you arrived at your choice."

The girl swiveled toward her, grateful for an appreciative audience. "I thought a lot about the questions you asked when you were helping me pick a chocolate."

"You mean," Abby said, trying to recall, "whether you like dark or milk chocolate, crunch or smooth, and the like?"

Maggie nodded. "Then I read your brochure."

"And based on that…."

"Based on that," she said, "I narrowed my criteria."

Once again, Abby resisted the urge to smile. She suspected that "narrowed my criteria" was a phrase Maggie had picked up from a grownup, probably her dad.

"And after you narrowed your criteria?"

"I picked the one with the most ingredients."

"Because…?"

"Because the one with the most ingredients is probably the one that's hardest to make."

"And you want the one that's hardest to make because…?"

"Because you'll be here. If we have questions, we can ask."

Abby blinked, surprised. She felt a rush of emotion. Maggie's ambition and logic reminded her so much of her younger self. "So don't keep me in suspense: Which one did you choose?"

Almost proudly, Maggie said, "The Crunchy Marshmallow Cherry Supreme."

"That's a great choice. You and Jacob have chosen well." With a smile, she pointed to a bowl. "We're going to start today's session with a batch of salted caramels, since they're a bit simpler to make, and from there we'll move on to the Cherry Supremes. For the caramels, we'll begin with the caramel itself, because it needs to cool down before we use it." She pointed to a printed recipe on the counter. "Jacob, can you read us the ingredients?"

Jacob picked up the piece of paper. "Water, sugar, salt, heavy cream, butter, and vanilla extract."

"Thank you." She gestured to the counter where she'd already set the ingredients. "Maggie, can you grab what we need? The cream is in the fridge."

As Maggie returned with the ingredients, Abby said, "Jacob, what do we do first?"

The boy consulted the recipe. "Combine the

water, salt, and sugar in a saucepan over medium heat."

"The saucepan's on the counter behind you," she said, then gestured to measuring utensils. "Maggie, why don't you add the water and salt while Jacob takes care of the sugar?"

As the kids focused on their tasks, Abby turned to John, who'd been watching with quiet approval. "While the kids tackle the caramel, it'd be great if you could get started on the chocolate."

"I'll get the double boiler going, then chop and melt the chocolate."

"Thanks."

Maggie added the sugar to the saucepan, watching her dad pour water into the pot and set it on the stove, and then grab a chocolate block, a cutting board, and a knife.

"Is he doing it right?" Maggie asked Abby quietly as her dad began chopping the chocolate into chunks.

"So far, so good," Abby replied with a smile, then turned to Jacob. "Next, for the caramel, we'll need a pastry brush."

Jacob returned seconds later. "Is this it?"

"That's it," Abby replied. "Dip the pastry brush in the water to get it wet, then brush the sides of the saucepan. We want to prevent sugar crystals from forming." Then, to Maggie, she said, "Can you get a second saucepan, add the cream to it, and warm it over a very low heat?"

"A very low heat?" Maggie repeated.

"We want the cream to warm up, but we don't want it to boil."

"Okay," the girl said, getting to work.

"The water is boiling," Jacob said.

"Perfect," Abby said. "John, how's the chocolate coming along?"

"Chopped and ready for melting."

"Kids," Abby said, "check the three chocolate piles your dad chopped up and let me know if the chunks are about a half-inch square. Also let me know if the three piles are about the same size."

The kids stepped closer to give the chocolate a critical eye.

"That's actually pretty good, Dad," Jacob said, surprised.

Maggie nodded in agreement. Abby could tell she was puzzled. "Dad, how did you know to make three piles?"

"It's in the recipe," he replied, then turned to Abby. "Time to start the melting?"

Abby nodded. "Jacob, what color is the water in the saucepan?"

"It's turning brown. Is that good?"

"That's very good. We want the sugared water to become amber in color. Time for a temperature check. Grab the thermometer over there on the counter. We're aiming for 320 degrees Fahrenheit."

Jacob retrieved the thermometer and dipped it in

the sugared water. "Why does the temperature matter?"

"The reason has to do with the sugar's chemistry. We want the dissolved sugar to start caramelizing."

"What does that mean?"

"'Caramelizing' means using heat to change the color of the sugar to brown." She pivoted to Maggie. "How's the cream warming up?"

"Okay, I think?"

"The temperature is 322," Jacob announced.

"Perfect. Time to lower the heat to medium low. Now, Maggie, I want you to slowly pour the cream into the sugared water, and then add the butter."

Maggie picked up the saucepan and held it over the other pan. "Slowly?"

"Yes, nice and slow. The cream will bubble and steam as it's added. It might splatter a bit — that's why it's important to be careful. Jacob, be ready to give the caramel a stir."

Cautiously, Maggie added the cream to the boiling liquid. As expected, the cream sputtered as Jacob stirred it in.

"Good job, you two. Maggie, we'll need to check the temperature again in about a minute. This time, we want the temperature to be 245 degrees Fahrenheit."

Abby watched the two kids work. In her experience, there was almost always a point in a class in which the students settled into their tasks — the moment when their distractions and nerves faded away and their flow became that of a well-oiled machine. Usually, that moment arrived later in the lesson.

But the twins had found their rhythm right away. Perhaps that's how they always were — naturally in sync.

She glanced at John and found him smiling at her, almost like he was reading her mind.

"How's the chocolate coming along?" she said.

He picked up a thermometer. "Almost the right temperature."

"How do you know the right temperature, Dad?" Maggie said.

"It's here in the recipe," he replied.

Maggie leaned over to confirm that, then looked again at her dad's face, as if sensing something was different about him but not able to pinpoint what.

Abby suppressed a smile as she watched Maggie trying to puzzle it out. "Maggie, how are we doing with the caramel temperature?"

The girl dipped the thermometer into the caramel, now a lovely amber. "It's 247."

"Great." Abby turned to Jacob. "Can you grab one of those big white bowls?"

While Jacob retrieved a bowl, Abby said, "Maggie, turn the burner off and carefully add the vanilla extract."

"Like this?" Maggie said as she added a capful.

"Yep. Stir it in — yes, that's good — and pour the caramel into the white bowl to cool."

Maggie did so, her movements assured, using a wooden spoon to get the last of the caramel out of the saucepan.

"How long do we let it cool?" Jacob asked, peering into the bowl.

"I usually allow the caramel to cool slowly on the counter, but we'll be needing it pretty soon, so today we'll speed things up by sticking it in the blast chiller."

"Where is that?"

Abby pointed. "Right over there."

"Abby," John said as he set the chocolate pot on the counter to cool, "the chocolate's ready, too."

"Perfect," she said as she gazed at three expectant faces. "Then you know what that means." She paused for a long second, aware that her students were eagerly awaiting her next words.

"Time for tempering!"

CHAPTER 16

*J*acob seemed intrigued — like he was having a better time than expected and was getting drawn into the process despite his initial reservations.

Maggie, in contrast, was positively giddy. "I've seen so many videos of this!" she gushed.

"Have you now?" Abby said with a laugh.

"What's tempering?" Jacob asked with a frown.

Briefly, Abby explained the science behind the technique, its importance in great chocolates, and the various ways in which things could go wrong.

She turned to John. "Can I ask you to demonstrate?"

The kids' eyes widened.

"Aren't you going to show us first?" Jacob asked carefully.

"No, I'd like your dad to show us."

With a grin, John grabbed the bowl of melted chocolate, held it poised dramatically over the marble countertop — and poured.

Jacob gasped as the chocolate spread over the marble. "You spilled it!"

"That's right," Abby said.

Fascinated, the kids watched John pick up a trowel and spread the chocolate over the surface. He worked it back together and spread it again, his movements displaying his natural affinity for this step.

"Here," he said to his daughter, handing her the trowel. "Your turn."

Tentatively at first but with increasing confidence, Maggie gave it a go, followed by Jacob.

As the afternoon progressed and the lesson continued, Abby showed them how to coat molds with the tempered chocolate, fill the molds with caramel using a piping bag, cover the caramel with a thin coating of chocolate, and sprinkle just the right amount of sea salt on top. She had them tackle the Crunchy Marshmallow Cherry Supreme next, giving them a chance to repeat many of the same steps and try some new ones as well.

She'd learned long ago that her students embraced their chocolate-making lessons in different ways. Most of her students were what she considered "enjoyers" — folks who signed up for the class to have a good time. For them, an afternoon in her kitchen was about being around lots of chocolate, eating lots of chocolate, and spending time with friends and family.

For other folks — the "artists," as Abby thought of them — making chocolate was a creative, even soulful, endeavor. They were passionate about learning and doing, and thought of food the same way Abby did — as a calling.

And then there were those who Abby termed the "chemists." In their own way, they were as passionate and committed as the artists. But for them, satisfaction came from understanding the process by which temperatures and techniques and ingredients combined to produce something beautiful and delicious.

Maggie was an artist through and through, her enthusiasm a joy to behold. Watching her was like watching a younger version of herself — full of passion, burning with a commitment to learn, eager to try everything she could. For her, the emotional connection was an essential ingredient.

Jacob, in contrast, was a chemist, his approach analytical and careful — excellent qualities for baking and chocolate-making, which tended to reward close attention to ingredients, timing, and technique. Abby found herself smiling as he measured a teaspoon of salt, eyeing the rim to ensure he had the exact amount. He didn't have the same level of interest in the culinary arts as his sister, she sensed, but he had respect for what they were doing here.

And John? She'd already learned he was a quick study. He most likely fell in the chemist camp, though she sensed a potential for artistry if and when inspiration struck — similar perhaps to architecture, where precision and creativity both came into play.

Very deliberately, Abby kept the pace of the class brisk to ensure her students had the opportunity to repeat the steps several times. Just as deliberately, as the class progressed, she stepped back to encourage her students to do more on their own.

A glance at the cuckoo clock confirmed what she already knew: Today's session was winding down. At the prep island, Maggie and Jacob were racing against time to complete a final batch of Cherry Supremes.

John joined her near a sink along the wall. Together, they watched the kids add caramel to a piping bag and start filling molds.

"They're great kids," she said.

"They are."

"Not sure you noticed," she murmured, "but Maggie is very aware of your newfound competence in the kitchen."

"Yep, definitely picked up on that," he said with a chuckle. "Don't worry, when they finish this batch, I'll give them the inside scoop on my amazing transformation."

"I'm not sold on your transformation being all that 'amazing,' by the way. I doubt you were ever as hopeless in the kitchen as you claim."

"Ha. On a different note, I have an idea how to keep James and Melody away from their house tomorrow afternoon. But I'll need your help."

Her heart rate quickened. "What's the idea?"

"The idea is for us to act like you're ready — actually, truly ready — to expand your kitchen."

She immediately saw where he was going. "So you'll…."

"I'll tell Melody I need James's input on architecture and construction questions, and I'll tell James you need Melody's advice on design questions."

"Which means both of them will be here at the shop —"

"Instead of up at the house."

"I like it," Abby said. "But one question: Who will be getting everything ready up at the workshop?"

"The mayor and his wife have volunteered their services."

"Perfect." With Bert and Elsie in charge of the final party prep, all was sure to go well. "That means all we have to do is…."

"Keep James and Melody occupied and away from home. And avoid spilling the beans about the double-surprise."

Jacob glanced up from his piping and noticed them talking, then whispered something to his sister.

Maggie said, loudly, "Dad and Abby, what are you two talking about?"

John said, "We're talking about the surprise party for James and Melody."

Jacob said, "Abby, are you helping, too?"

"I am," Abby said.

Maggie added, "Is that how you know each other?"

Abby said, "You mean, have I been helping your dad plan the party?"

Maggie nodded and held her gaze, waiting for an answer. She didn't seem upset or concerned — but she definitely seemed curious.

"That's one of the reasons Abby and I have gotten to know each other," John said. "But there's another reason as well."

The two kids went still. Jacob joined his sister in looking up at his dad, waiting for what he was going to say.

John cleared his throat. "I've been taking lessons from Abby in chocolate-making."

"Lessons?" Maggie said, her brow furrowing. "When?"

"The past two Wednesday evenings."

Her eyes widened. "When Grandma and Grandpa made dinner?" When he nodded, she asked, "Why did you take lessons?"

"Well," he said. "I wanted to do better in the kitchen."

"You're definitely doing better in the kitchen," Jacob said.

"Dad," Maggie said, her voice starting to tremble, "why do you want to do better in the kitchen?"

John approached his daughter and knelt in front of her. "Because I want us to do more together. Jacob and I have hockey. For you and me…. I'm hoping we can make great things together in the kitchen."

Maggie's eyes filled with tears. She rushed into his arms. "We can, Dad, we can. We'll bake the best things ever."

"Good," he said with a laugh, pulling her in tight. "I can't wait."

"Let's make a cake. A huge chocolate cake."

"That sounds great."

Maggie's gaze darted to Abby. "Did you show him how to make a chocolate cake?"

"Sorry, we didn't get to that," Abby said with a laugh, "but I've seen him in the kitchen and I know he'll do a great job."

John swiveled toward Jacob. "You can join us too, buddy."

"Okay," Jacob said, clearly pleased to be included. Then he glanced at Abby. "Abby, what about you? Do you want to come over sometime and help us?"

A feeling of warmth flowed through Abby — there was such a hopeful tone in Jacob's voice. "I'd like that very much, Jacob."

When he beamed at her, Maggie said, "Abby, do you make chocolate other-things?"

"Other things? Like…?"

"Like chocolate cake?"

"Every once in a while. In fact, I'm making a chocolate cake for tomorrow's party."

"You're like Heartsprings Valley's queen of chocolate," Maggie said.

Abby laughed. "I don't know about 'queen,'" she said modestly, "but I'm definitely a fan of all the wonderful things we can do with the beans of the cacao plant."

The girl grinned at her. "Well, I'm definitely a fan of *yours*!"

"Me, too," Jacob added.

"Make that three," John added, the green in his eyes flashing.

"You three are embarrassing me," Abby said with a smile, heat rushing to her cheeks. "I've had so much fun with you today. Now it's time for you to scoot on home."

CHAPTER 17

*A*bby's smile refused to leave her face, even after she shooed John and the kids out of the kitchen loaded with all the chocolates they'd made that afternoon. John had offered to help clean up, but Abby had firmly said no and given each of the kids a hug goodbye.

That night, after a long evening in her shop making James's surprise chocolate cake and boxing up Melody's order of surprise chocolates, Abby collapsed into bed and fell into yet another vivid dream. This time, she found herself in a home she didn't recognize, in a living room at Christmas. On the mantel above the lovely fireplace, holiday decorations were hung with care. In the corner stood a big tree festooned with lights and ornaments. She breathed in the welcoming scent of freshly baked gingerbread cookies, wafting in from the kitchen.

She felt a tug on her hand and found a little girl — a very determined little girl — trying to pull her toward the front door. The girl was about five, with big brown eyes and shoulder-length brown hair.

"Grandma," she was saying. "You promised."

"I promised what?" Abby replied, even as she realized the little girl's words made no sense. Why was this girl calling her *Grandma*?

"You promised to build a snowman with me," the girl said. "Remember?"

Abby remembered no such thing — how could she, since she had no memory of anything related to any of this? A glance through the living room windows told her she was in Heartsprings Valley, in a house on a street a few blocks from hers. Fresh snow blanketed the ground, glistening in the bright afternoon sun.

"A snowman sounds perfect," she found herself saying to the little girl. "But first we have to get you bundled up."

The girl dashed off to grab her things, leaving Abby with a feeling of warmth and contentment and a powerful rush of love that came from knowing — somehow, without understanding how or why — that this little girl was *right*. She, Abby Donovan, was this girl's *grandmother*.

"Bingo," a familiar voice said behind her.

Abby whirled around to find Clara, dressed head to toe in a festive Santa suit. "Clara," she gasped.

"What is this? I'm in another one of my crazy dreams, aren't I?"

"Bingo again." Her friend pulled her in for a quick hug, then stepped back and did a twirl. "I wasn't sure about the Santa gear, but I have to say, I'm seeing the possibilities. What's the verdict?"

"Very festive," Abby replied, trying to calm her beating heart. "Where are we?"

"You mean, *when* are we."

"When?"

"Right."

"Okay. *When* are we?"

"Twenty years out, I think. Maybe twenty-five?" Clara peered closely at Abby's face. "You're holding up really well, by the way. Your skin looks fantastic."

Abby quelled a surge of exasperation. "Clara, what's going on?"

"I can't tell you that," she said regretfully. "Dem's da rules. But you're a smart cookie. I know you'll figure it out."

"Figure out what?"

"What you need to do when you wake up." Clara took a deep breath, as if steeling herself, then stepped closer. "Okay, Abby, crunch time. Big decisions coming. Life choices that affect not just you, but people you haven't even met yet."

"Like this little girl?"

"Especially this little girl."

"How can this girl be my granddaughter? I have no children of my own."

"True enough." Clara clearly wanted to say more but was holding back.

Abby sighed. "I suppose this is one of the things I need to figure out?"

"Right again. Okay, take my hand."

Abby eyed her warily. "Why?"

"More to see. Places and times to go. One thing to warn you about. What's coming next is jumbled. There's no order to it — it's not at all how I would handle it. But I'm not the organizer here, just the messenger."

"I'm not following."

"I know, and I'm sorry. All I can say is, everything you're about to see is related."

"Related in what way?"

"All of it depends on *you*."

Abby gulped with apprehension. "What are you saying, Clara?"

"Sorry, I've already blabbed too much." She extended her hand. "Clock's a-ticking. Grab hold."

With a mixture of foreboding and curiosity, Abby took hold of Clara's hand and —

She was outside. It was night. Snow was falling, the flakes thick and soft. She was sitting in a sleigh, her legs tucked beneath a thick wool blanket.

There was a horse in front of her — a big brown

beauty who turned her head to greet her, her soft eyes gentle and welcoming.

She wasn't alone in the sleigh, she realized. A man was seated on the bench next to her. She couldn't see his face, but his solid presence felt familiar and reassuring.

The man gave the reins a confident flick and the horse snorted eagerly in response.

And they were off!

The sleigh flew across a field of fresh-fallen snow into a bank of misty fog that parted to reveal a house decorated for Christmas. Effortlessly, the sleigh passed through the home's front windows and into the dining room, where a family was gathered around a table loaded with turkey and other holiday treats. Abby couldn't make out the faces, but somehow she knew she was witnessing two teenagers, two grandparents, and a husband and wife, all gabbing away merrily. The sleigh moved past them, through more mist, into a hospital room, where she saw herself — an older version of herself, that is — holding a newborn in her arms, the baby's mom gazing up at her from the hospital bed with love and pride. More scenes flashed by, faster and faster. She saw herself in the stands at the town's ice rink, cheering on the high school hockey team. Then she found herself in another scene, watching herself step onto a stage to accept a judge's ribbon, the audience applauding loudly. And then, from across a crowded restaurant, she saw a man drop to his knees before a woman. She couldn't tell who the man and woman were — the scene was blurry, like she was witnessing it through a filter. The man gazed up at the woman. From his coat pocket he pulled out a ring box and opened it, revealing a sparkling diamond. "Will you marry me?" he said. And from across the room, she heard the woman, with a voice that sounded just like her own, whisper, "Yes."

Gasping, Abby awoke with a start, heart racing. She bolted upright and glanced around desperately.

Yes yes *yes*, she realized, relief flooding through her. She was in her own bed, safe and sound at home. Gratefully, she dropped back onto her pillow. Yet another crazy dream. What on earth was going on? Clearly her subconscious was revved into overdrive and roaring away. That had to be what was going on. What other logical explanation could there be?

Technicolor visions like these — suggestive and encouraging, fanciful and puzzling — happened all the time to other people, she told herself. They were nothing to worry about or concern herself with or even give much thought to.

Yet their vividness was startling. And the way they seemed to be giving her advance warning of what was coming....

Nonsense, she told herself.

As before, the ideal course of action was to defer any digging until later. Today would be yet another jam-packed day. The double-surprise party started at six. John was bringing Melody and James to the chocolate shop at four-thirty. With Christmas drawing near, the shop would be inundated with shoppers from the moment she opened at eleven. And before that — story of her life — she had batches and batches of chocolates to make.

With a determined groan, she swung her feet out of bed and rose to begin her busy day.

CHAPTER 18

*A*s Abby had predicted, the day descended on her like a nonstop train. The hours flew by, and almost before she knew it, it was time for John to show up with Melody and James.

Right on time, the shop door opened and the three of them stepped in. Abby realized she hadn't seen James in over a month — crazy how busy things were. He was a big, handsome guy, tall and broad-shouldered, with a head of thick brown hair and a beard flecked with grey, dressed as usual in work boots, jeans, and flannel shirt. Though Melody was also on the tall side, next to him she almost seemed petite.

Abby bustled up to greet them, then went to the front door and flipped the "Open" sign to "Closed."

"So glad you're all here," she said. "Please, step into the kitchen."

"I am so thrilled you're expanding," Melody said.

"Same here," James said as he ran his eyes over the walls and ceiling.

"Ditto," Abby said. Quickly, she ran through her wish list, James and Melody listening intently.

"Darling," Melody said when she finished. "I love all of it. Your dream kitchen sounds wonderful."

"My worry is that I might be biting off more than I can chew. That's why I'm hoping for advice."

James turned to John. "Tell me about the roof and the foundation."

"Let me show you," John said.

The two men headed out back and Abby was about to follow when Melody signaled for her to wait. "John has done a fabulous job with the party planning," Melody whispered excitedly as soon as the men were out of hearing range. "Bert and Elsie are up at the workshop right now, getting everything ready." She giggled. "And the best part is — James doesn't suspect a thing. He's in for such a surprise!"

"That's great," Abby said with a smile. *And he's not the only one.*

"The idea you had to rent the school's big yellow bus and have the guests meet in the school parking lot and drive up to the house together? Pure genius. When we drive up, there won't be a car in sight."

Abby glanced toward the back door. "So how do you want this to play out? Do you want me to ask if I can check out the workshop space?"

"That would be perfect. Tell James you want to learn more about what John's doing with insulation or heating or some such."

The two men stepped back inside. James rubbed his hands together. "Brrr — it's a cold one today."

"What's your take on all this?" Abby asked.

"John's definitely onto something. What he's talking about seems both feasible and affordable."

"Oh, perfect," Melody said.

John gestured to the sketches he'd brought. "Why don't we run through these and see what questions come up?"

As the four of them crowded around the sketches and dove into a detailed discussion, Abby found herself marveling at how perfectly John had managed to capture the essence of what she'd been dreaming about. Clearly he'd listened closely; her future kitchen seemed to come to vivid life as he walked them through the plan.

She could have kept going with the kitchen talk forever, but a glance at the clock told her it was time to get Melody and James up to the workshop for their double-surprise.

"You know," she said, "I'd love to learn more about the flooring you mentioned." She turned to Melody. "This might be an imposition, but would it be okay if we drove up to the workshop to check it out?"

"You mean right now?" Melody asked, playing her part.

"Would that be okay?"

"I don't see why not." Melody turned to James. "Is that all right, darling?"

"Sure, sounds great. John, want to join us?"

"I'd love to."

As they got bundled up, James pulled Abby aside and whispered, "Thanks again for helping with the surprise." He glanced at Melody, a gleam in his eyes. "She doesn't have a clue!"

"Glad I was able to help," Abby whispered. *And by the way, James, your wife isn't the only one in for a surprise.*

A few minutes later, Abby ushered everyone out and locked up. She shivered beneath her scarf — James was right about it being cold.

"Hop in," James said, gesturing to his SUV parked across the street. Abby climbed up into the back seat, John following, and before they knew it they were off, Melody chattering away happily in the front seat, regaling them with tidbits from the movie she'd just finished filming.

The Victorian mansion that Melody had bought, renovated, and now called home stood on the ridge overlooking Heartsprings Valley, on five acres of land at the end of a twisty road about ten minutes outside of town. When they reached the gravel driveway, James wound them through a grove of pine trees that opened onto a wide meadow. Across the meadow stood the restored house, grandly revealed. It seemed to glow in the dark, crisply white against the surrounding trees, like something out of a dream — a Hollywood version of a Victorian fantasy, its spires and turrets and decorative elements creating drama and interest from every angle.

James pulled to a stop out front. The night was quiet and still.

Across the meadow, Abby spotted a one-story structure nestled among the trees. "Is that it?"

"That's it," James said.

"Almost finished," Melody added.

They made their way along a path across the meadow past a gazebo that Melody had recently installed for warm-weather outdoor gatherings. Abby pointed to the workshop's wide garage door next to the regular door. "Is that so you can move furniture out?"

"And lumber and supplies in," James said.

John slid a key into the lock and pushed opened the door. "James and Melody, after you."

"I can't wait to see the latest updates," Melody said cheerfully.

Abby followed James and Melody inside. John shut the door behind them. For a few seconds, they stood in the quiet workshop, blanketed in darkness.

"I'll hit the light," John said.

Then, with a flip of a switch —

Light flooded the workshop and a crowd of excited faces yelled —

"SURPRISE!"

Melody and James both laughed out loud and turned to each other, waiting for the other to express utter shock.

And then, as it became clear to both of them that neither of them was surprised — and that each of them was expecting the other to be surprised — they both whirled toward John.

"Buddy," James began, "what's going on?"

Comprehension dawned in Melody's eyes. "Darling," she said, turning to her husband. "Is this party supposed to be a surprise for *me*?"

"To celebrate wrapping the movie," James said — and then he seemed to get a glimmer as well. "So wait, are you saying *you* threw this party to surprise *me*?"

"That's right, darling, to celebrate the opening of the workshop."

They stared at each other, eyes wide and mouths open, then both swiveled again to John, who gave them a big grin and said:

"Double surprise!"

James and Melody erupted in laughter and the room cheered as the happy couple hugged and kissed.

Melody cried out, her stage voice carrying effortlessly across the crowded room, "Best double-surprise party ever!"

Bert stepped up to assume his mayoral duties and announced, "Everyone, let's get this party started. And don't forget, we're collecting donations for the Christmas charity drive. Be prepared to be generous!"

Abby gazed happily at her friends. The surprise had worked! Melody and James were both delighted. And Bert and Elsie and their helpers had done an amazing job getting everything ready. Wreaths decorated every wall, tinsel and ornaments were draped over every worktable and woodworking machine, and tables loaded with drinks and treats were set up throughout the room. Over the speakers, the town's radio station was playing a melodic reminder that Santa Claus was coming to town.

Abby scanned the crowd, pleased to see so many familiar faces. In a corner, she spied Betsy and Don with Maggie and Jacob.

Abby waved to them and Maggie rushed over.

"Abby," she said excitedly. "Did you make the chocolate cake on the table over there?"

"I did."

Without warning, Maggie gave her a big hug. "It looks soooo good! Can you show us how to make it?"

"Of course," Abby said with a laugh.

Jacob joined them, looking like he wanted a hug,

too. "Maybe you can come to our house?" he asked, his voice hopeful. "We live pretty close."

"I'd love to, Jacob," she said, pulling him in for a quick embrace as well.

Both kids beamed up at her, gratified and excited.

Another kid rushed up, breathless. "Jacob and Maggie, a bunch of us are going to the big house to play hide-and-seek!"

The kids' eyes lit up. "Can we?" Jacob asked, turning to John.

"Over at the house?" John said. "That's up to Melody and James."

At the sound of her name, Melody turned around. "What's up to me and James?"

"The kids have a request," John said.

Maggie and Jacob and their young friend exchanged a look, and their friend said, his voice trembling, "Ms. Connelly, can we play hide-and-seek in your house?"

"Of course you can," Melody said immediately. "The front door's open — head on in. There's just one rule." She leaned down to face the kids directly. "And that rule is: Have fun!"

With whoops of delight, the kids rushed off.

"Oh, and don't break anything!" she yelled merrily as they dashed away.

Bert, who'd been listening, seemed mildly apprehensive. "You realize what you've done."

"What's that?"

"You've opened your doors to a wild stampeding horde."

"Oh, they'll be fine," Melody said with a laugh, even as a shadow of a doubt crossed her brow. "Right?"

John cleared his throat. "How about I go chaperone? Any areas of the house off-limits?"

"Thank you, John, that sounds perfect. The little munchkins can hide themselves anywhere they please."

Abby was about to offer to join him when she spied Tucker, the young man from the job-training center, across the room. He was frowning at a table loaded with treats and looking like he needed help.

"John," she said, "I have to check on the treats table. How about if I join you at the house in a few?"

"I'd love the company," he said, the green in his eyes flashing. "See you there."

She watched him head out after the kids, then made her way to the treats table, the smile on her face refusing to fade.

"Tucker," she said. "Good to see you."

"Abby," he replied, a grin lighting up his face. "Great party."

"It's turned out well. I take it you're a friend of…."

"James. We worked on a couple of projects together this year." He returned his attention to the table. "Mayor Winters asked if I could move the table a bit to the left, but it's got so much stuff on it, I'm not sure how to…."

Abby joined him in assessing the situation. "The pies and cakes will be fine, but that stack of cookies will slip-slide away if we try to move it."

"Exactly."

"Let's try anyway. If we shift the cookies and that jar of candy canes to the center of the table…."

"Got it." Working together, they repositioned plates to minimize slippage, then grabbed opposite ends of the table and slowly scooted it to the desired spot.

"The mayor said the sight lines are better here," Tucker explained.

Abby quickly saw the mayor was right. From this spot, the table was directly visible from the front door. "Bert knows events like nobody's business."

A voice behind her called her name and she turned to find Anna approaching with a big grin. "Congrats on pulling this off."

Abby smiled and shook her head. "John deserves the credit, not me."

Anna shook her head cheerfully. "I know how much you helped, so sorry, I'm totally not buying that."

Abby introduced her to Tucker, then returned her attention to the table. "I should probably get some of that cake sliced and on plates…."

"I can handle that," Anna said.

"I'll help," Tucker added.

"Okay," Abby said, "I'll leave you two to it." With a smile, she pivoted and was about to make her way to the main house when —

A vision from her unconscious appeared.

Shock rolled through her.

Approaching her was an impossibility.

It couldn't be.

She gasped with astonishment. Slipping toward her through the crowd were Gail, Hettie Mae, and Clara — decked out in matching Santa Claus outfits.

Just like in her dreams!

CHAPTER 19

Stunned, Abby spluttered, "You three are...." She couldn't even finish the thought. "What are you doing in...?"

Hettie Mae laughed and did a twirl. "Fun, isn't it? When Clara suggested we dress up like this, I almost said no. But I have to say, I'm having a grand old time."

Gail laughed. "Definitely out of normal for me, too. But hey, when the mood strikes...."

Clara was beaming. "It's just our way of celebrating the Christmas spirit."

Abby felt faint. What she was seeing was *impossible*. "Did you say Christmas spirit?" she repeated.

"Abby," Gail said, "are you okay? You seem pale."

"I'm fine," Abby said automatically, trying to

recover. "I'm just … surprised to see you all in Santa suits."

The trio wasn't aware of her vivid dreams — she hadn't told anyone about them. Yet here they were, dressed just like they had been in her head….

Coincidence, she tried to tell herself. It had to be.

"You know, this could be the start of a new Christmas tradition," Clara said, eyeing the others to gauge their interest. "We pick a day during the holiday season and agree to go full Santa."

"I'm in," Hettie Mae said with a laugh.

"Same here," Gail chimed in.

Clara turned to Abby. "How about you?"

Abby blinked, still recovering from the shock of seeing her friends dressed this way. "How about me what?"

"Are you on board for a day of Santa suit fun next year?"

A smile crept to Abby's lips. Coincidence or not, the three of them were clearly having a ball. "Of course. Count me in."

"Excellent," Clara said, rubbing her hands together, her eyes bright with enthusiasm. "That settles it. Next year's Santa Day is going to be *huge*."

Abby laughed. Given Clara's organizing prowess, she'd probably convince the entire town to dress up.

Hettie Mae was casting her gaze around the workshop. "Where are little Maggie and Jacob? Frank and I leave for our cruise in two days. I brought them their Christmas presents."

"They're with the other kids and John at the main house," Abby said. "Hide-and-seek, I think."

At the mention of John's name, Abby noticed three pairs of eyes swivel toward her.

"You know," Hettie Mae said, very casually, "I've always liked John. He's a lot like Don. Solid, smart, dependable."

"Good-looking, too," Clara threw in.

"Seems like a great guy and a great dad," Gail added.

Her friends' intent couldn't have been clearer. And while normally Abby would have brushed aside their attempted meddling with ease, this time was different, because this time….

She felt her cheeks flush.

Hettie Mae noticed immediately, of course — she always did. "Elsie was right," she said with satisfaction.

Abby went still. "Right about what?"

Hettie Mae glanced briefly at Clara and Gail, then pointed behind Abby. "Best you let her tell you." Abby followed Hettie Mae's finger and her eyes landed on Elsie at the treats table, where she was helping herself to a healthy slice of the double-chocolate cake.

Abby frowned. What exactly was Elsie right about? She swung her attention back to her Santaclad friends and saw they'd chosen that moment to abandon her and were already halfway across the room, clearly determined to avoid answering any further questions.

With a sigh that came from being extremely aware of how Heartsprings Valley operated, Abby slipped through the crowd and joined Elsie, who'd found a quiet corner and was about to dig into her cake.

"Evening, Elsie."

"Lovely party, Abby," her friend said, then pointed toward her plate. "I was so glad to see your cake here. You know I can't resist."

"Thank you." Abby squared her shoulders. "So the girls just told me you're right."

"Did they now? Right about what?"

"Well," Abby said. "That's what I'd like you to tell me."

"I see." Elsie took a bite of the cake. "Mmm, so good." After a pause, she added, "Yes, I suppose it's time you know."

"Know what?"

"How this came about."

"How what came about?"

"This," Elsie said simply, gesturing toward the crowded party. "And yes, it was my idea. Most of it, at least. In case you need someone to blame."

"Your idea?" Abby replied, now thoroughly confused.

Elsie nodded simply, holding Abby's gaze with

her patient grey eyes. There was no pretense about Elsie. In language, tone, and appearance, her friend nearly always came across as calmness personified. She didn't get ruffled. She didn't stir up fusses. Instead she listened and observed and, when her help was required, she acted. In her own quiet way, she was very much the town's co-mayor, supporting Bert's efforts to promote and strengthen the town they both loved.

Abby pushed back a wave of emotion. "Why did you…?"

"Set all this in motion?" Elsie said, nodding again to the jam-packed room. "It seemed like the right thing to do, especially after what Betsy told me."

"What did Betsy tell you?"

"She said John was ready to start dating again but didn't know it."

Abby tensed, confused. What did the party have to do with John being ready to date? "And so…."

"Betsy said she wanted him to meet the right person. Someone who would be a good fit for him and the kids."

A jumble of emotions stirred within her. "So you…."

"So I sent Betsy to your shop."

Abby froze. "My shop? Why?"

"Because you're wonderful, dear."

Abby wasn't going to let the compliment sidetrack her. "What exactly was your purpose in sending Betsy to my shop?"

"To check you out."

"To check me out?" Abby repeated, taken aback by how matter-of-factly Elsie said it.

"Oh, come now. How else was I going to get her on board?"

"On board?"

"For the plan," Elsie said patiently. She gave Abby a puzzled look, as if surprised she needed to explain this to her.

So there was a plan. Abby took a deep breath and willed herself to be calm. Clearly there was a lot she didn't know. "Tell me about the plan."

Elsie took another bite of the chocolate cake. "I could eat this all day. So good. Now, where was I?"

"The plan. You sent Betsy to the shop...."

"Do you remember Betsy visiting the shop back in November, before Thanksgiving?"

"Yes."

"She called me afterward and said you seemed so nice and gave me the go-ahead." Elsie took another bite. "Mmm, so rich. You should make this more often."

"Thank you," Abby said, trying not to show her impatience. "Getting back to the plan...."

"It takes two to tango, of course," Elsie said reflectively. "So the real question was, how were we going to get you and John onto the same dance floor?"

"Meaning…?"

"You're both so busy and focused. All you do is make chocolates in your shop and go home and sleep — wash, rinse, repeat. John's no better, spending all of his time with his clients or his kids. If the plan was going to have a prayer of succeeding, we knew we'd have to get you two to meet each other."

"So you…."

"And it needed to be more than just a crossing of paths, mind you. You needed to spend time together. Luckily, Maggie's interest in chocolate-making showed us the way."

Abby shook her head with wonder. The outlines of the plan were becoming apparent. As always, the meddling expertise of the people in this town was off the charts. "So Betsy encouraged John to sign up himself and the kids for my chocolate-making class."

"That was Part One."

The plan had multiple parts? The scheme was getting more complicated by the second. "And Part Two?"

"The private lessons, of course," Elsie said. "Betsy's husband Don had a heart-to-heart with John about father-daughter bonding. Then Betsy reminded John how disaster-prone he was in the kitchen and suggested private lessons to help him prepare."

"About that," Abby said, feeling an urge to defend him, "John's really not a disaster in the kitchen. He's actually quite competent."

Elsie smiled gently. "Good thing he hadn't realized that yet."

Abby struggled to keep her expression and tone neutral, determined to fully understand the plan. "So Betsy roped Don into the scheme."

"That's right."

"And Betsy used John's concerns about his kitchen skills...."

"To encourage him to call you and ask for private lessons."

"How did he know I offer private lessons?"

"We told him," Elsie said.

Abby swallowed back another rush of emotion. "So what I'm hearing, Elsie, is that you used John's love for his daughter to maneuver him into doing something he never would have thought of doing on his own."

"Exactly," Elsie said with a pleased smile.

"Doesn't that seem ... manipulative?"

"Oh, very much so," Elsie said. "But it's for a good cause, so who's to complain?"

Me, she almost said. Instead she said, "You're incorrigible."

"John was the easy half of this, of course."

Abby went still. "You manipulated me, too?"

Elsie's gaze was kind. "'Manipulate' — such a negative-sounding word. I prefer 'encourage.'"

Again, Abby had to resist the impulse to object. "What form did your 'encouragement' take?"

"That was Part Three of the plan. The surprise party for James and Melody, of course."

Abby blinked — she hadn't seen that coming. Puzzled, she glanced around the crowded workshop. "How does the party factor in?"

"Well," Elsie said gently, "to answer that question, we have to talk about *you*."

"Me?"

"Yes." Elsie took a deep breath. "I hope I can speak frankly?"

"Of course," Abby replied, suddenly apprehensive.

Elsie set her cake on a nearby table to give Abby her full and undivided attention. "You, Abby Donovan, are a determined, focused, hardworking, generous, caring woman. You're also stubborn and at times too cautious. These qualities, all of them, have been important to your business success, but they're also why you're so resistant to change."

Reluctantly, under Elsie's kind but firm gaze, Abby found herself nodding in agreement. The connection with the party still wasn't apparent, but she didn't want to interrupt her friend.

Elsie continued. "Plus, you're sharp. We knew you'd see through any of the usual approaches."

"Usual approaches? You mean … matchmaking ploys?"

"For example, inviting you and John over for dinner and sitting you next to each other."

"Nothing wrong with a good dinner party. That could have been nice."

"I'm sure you're right. But would it have worked?"

Abby was about to argue that it might have, but then found herself pausing.

"Yes," Elsie said, as if reading her mind. "You would have seen instantly what I was up to, and you're stubbornly allergic to being set up. You married the wrong man after your friends pushed you toward him. Now your hackles go up whenever someone tries the same."

Abby blinked at the truth in Elsie's words. "Yet you just admitted to doing the very thing I'm allergic to."

"Except this time, you didn't know about the pushing."

"I don't see how that changes anything."

"Don't you?" Elsie said mildly. "As far as you knew, the only thing going on was that you agreed to give John private lessons. You weren't being set up. You weren't being encouraged by anyone. Which meant you had nothing to be resentful or defensive about. Nothing for your hackles to rise up and put a stop to."

Before Abby could reply, Elsie added, "There's also the time element."

"Meaning…?"

"Let's pretend for a moment that I hosted that

dinner party you mentioned and invited the two of you. Let's say the two of you hit it off, and one of you worked up the courage to ask the other on a date. How much time would pass before your busy schedules allowed that date? I can imagine you telling him you couldn't meet until after the Christmas rush."

Again, Abby found herself nodding.

"That wasn't going to be good enough. No, we wanted the two of you to spend time together now, not later."

"Why now?"

"Because when it comes to getting to know someone, now is nearly always better than later."

Again, Abby found herself accepting the older woman's wisdom.

"Plus," Elsie continued, "how does one navigate all of those silly rules of dating in this day and age? Goodness, there are so many. And they seem to require so much effort."

"Effort?"

"I'm no expert, mind you, but I hear things. It seems complicated. Especially the first date. You need to schedule the date a certain number of days in advance. If you agree to go to a restaurant or movie or some such, you drive there separately. You have a friend call during the date to give you an easy excuse to leave in case the date isn't going well. And so on."

"You're not wrong," Abby admitted.

"Even when you actually succeed in clearing these hurdles, the real question is: How much time do you actually spend together? Two hours? If the date's going well, perhaps three?"

"I don't see why...."

"No, you do see why. You met John two weeks ago. In that time, you've spent — how much time with him? Eight hours? Nine? Ten?"

Abby inhaled sharply as she realized what Elsie was saying. "And in the time we've spent together...."

"You've gotten to know each other. In a faster way — a better way — than the regular dating rules allow."

"So you...."

Elsie reached for her cake and took another bite. "Now where was I? I realized that, if we wanted you two to spend time together, we needed to go after you through your business."

Abby's breath caught. The way Elsie phrased it — "go after you through your business" — sounded so *ruthless*.

"Of course," Elsie said, "there's no way to predict chemistry. Sometimes it's there, sometimes it's not. So even if you two hadn't hit it off, we wanted something good to come out it for both of you."

"Good for us how?"

"Professionally."

Abby blinked again. Elsie had really thought through this plan of hers.

Elsie continued. "You've been unhappy at work for a while now. You feel stuck in the same old routine, doing the same old thing, day in, day out. You feel stale. And that's never good."

"So your thought was that, even if we didn't hit it off…."

"John is an architect who works with small businesses, and you're a small businesswoman who needs a bigger kitchen."

"Okay, I get that. But the surprise party? I still don't see how…."

"Oh, that's easy," Elsie said calmly. "The party was insurance, plain and simple. An extra reason for you two to spend time together."

"So…." Abby's voice trailed off as she tried to connect all the dots. "How did you manage that part of it? When you got invited to the party, you decided to…?"

Again, Elsie seemed surprised. "Surely you don't need me to explain."

Abby stared at her friend, still not following. Then, very slowly, the truth dawned. "You're telling me that James and Melody were part of this plan of yours."

Elsie nodded. "Melody was excited, of course — she loves a good party. And James was such a dear, moving around his client appointments in L.A. to make sure he was available to call you during your first private lesson with John."

"Wait," Abby said, still catching up, determined to make sure she fully understood. "They were in on your plan from the get-go?"

"Oh, yes."

"You mean, when Melody showed up in my shop and told me she wanted to surprise James, she was carrying out your plan?"

"That's right, dear."

"And James was also...?" Her voice trailed off. "So you're saying the surprise party — I'm sorry, the *double*-surprise party — really wasn't a surprise for James and Melody at all?"

"No, not for James and Melody," Elsie said gently.

Abby breathed in sharply as the implications sank in.

That meant....

She cast her gaze around the crowded workshop. Across the room, she spied their hosts, arm in arm, wine glasses in hand, murmuring to each other and laughing, so very much in love. James noticed Abby's gaze and whispered in his wife's ear. Melody glanced over and threw Abby an excited, conspiratorial smile. Then they raised their glasses and toasted her from afar, their faces glowing with affection.

Abby felt her face flush. Without warning, tears

threatened. She turned back to Elsie. "That means you — all of you — did this for...."

Elsie set her cake down again, then took hold of Abby's hands and gripped them tightly. Her voice was soft and full of love as she said:

"Yes, dear. We did all of this for *you*."

CHAPTER 20

The tears Abby found herself blinking back weren't from sadness — quite the opposite — but rather from an overwhelming rush of surprise and gratitude. Her dear friends, who knew her so well and cared for her so much, had gone above and beyond to give her a chance at what they knew she was ready to embrace once again.

"You are truly impossible," she whispered. "All of you." Then she pulled Elsie in for a hug. "Thank you."

As Elsie squeezed her tight, Abby realized she no longer had a choice, not after the lengths her friends had gone to. Their careful planning had successfully thwarted her instinctive defensiveness and resistance. Now she owed them. For her sake and theirs, she needed to see their plan through.

A tremor of longing and anticipation swept through her.

When Elsie finally let her go, Abby gazed at the wise woman who had oh-so-meticulously guided the whole plan. "I don't know what I'd do without you in my life."

Elsie smiled. "I feel the same about you, dear."

"I'm so lucky to have you as my friend. This entire town is lucky to have you as their friend."

"You know what to do, right?"

Abby brushed back a tear. "I guess so? I'm awfully rusty."

"So is he. Don't you worry about that." She gestured toward the door. "You know where he is, right?"

Abby nodded. "No time like the present?"

"That's the spirit. Now go get him." Then Elsie picked up her plate and slipped away into the crowd.

Abby took a deep breath, trying to calm her rapidly beating heart. Before she could talk herself out of it, she made her way to the workshop door and out into the cold night. Overhead, a canopy of stars twinkled. As the workshop door closed behind her, the party hubbub faded to a murmur. Her boots crunched softly as she crossed the open meadow to the main house, her breath turning to mist in the frigid air.

Dashing up to the front porch, she pushed open the big main door and stepped into the welcoming embrace of the home's excellent heating. From somewhere upstairs, she heard the patter of foot-steps and the excited yells of hide-and-seekers at play.

Was John upstairs? Or was he —

"Abby," she heard him say. She whirled around and found him gazing at her from the entrance to the living room.

"Hey," she said, her heart thumping at the sight of him. "Sounds like the kids are having fun."

He grinned. "This place is perfect for that. Lots of nooks and crannies."

She joined him in the living room, her gaze lingering briefly on the gorgeous Christmas tree standing proud next to the big back windows. "Any of the kids hiding down here?"

"They're doing it by floor. They started down in the basement and just did a round here on the main level. Now they're trying out the second and third floors."

He was so handsome standing there in his crisp blue shirt. From the way he was gazing at her, it was clear he was glad she'd joined him.

Now's the time, Abby. Ignoring the knot in her stomach, she stepped closer and cleared her throat. "Since we have the room to ourselves, at least for the moment, there's something I'd like to say."

She looked up into his patient, kind eyes. Already she felt safer and surer of herself. "There are two questions I'd like to ask. But first, I have something to share."

His focus was steady and clear. "I'm listening."

She took a deep breath — *you can do this* — and willed herself to speak calmly. "For the past year, I've been at a crossroads, personally and professionally." The instant the words left her mouth, she could feel her tension easing. "On the professional side, I've been dreaming for a while now about expanding my business, but I've been holding back, mindful of what that entails. My life is already crazy-busy, and the prospect of committing to even more work has been, frankly, terrifying."

He nodded, encouraging her to continue.

"And then there's me, at a personal crossroads. For eight years, I've devoted every ounce of energy to my chocolates and my shop and my customers. I love what I do, and I love what I already have in my life, but I've come to realize that what I have isn't enough — not any longer. I want *more*. But until recently, I had no idea how to go after that."

His voice was thick with emotion. "What happened recently?"

"You happened," she said, the words coming so much more easily than expected, carried on a wave of relief that she was finally expressing herself. "I met you. And through meeting you, I realized something important."

He stepped forward and took hold of her hands,

his skin warm to the touch, his eyes electric with feeling. "What did you realize, Abby?"

"Since moving to Heartsprings Valley, my purpose in life has been about proving to myself that I'm strong enough and determined enough to take on a big challenge. And what I've realized is — I've done that. I've accomplished that. I've shown myself that, with hard work and perseverance, I can make my dreams come true."

He nodded, waiting for her to continue.

"Which means the next part of my journey doesn't need to be about proving myself to myself. The next part of my journey can be about something more."

"Something more?" he repeated, urging her onward.

"I mentioned I had two questions for you," she said softly.

His gaze intensified. "Ask away."

"The first is a professional question. I've decided to expand my kitchen, and for that, I need a really great architect." In a softly playful tone, she added, "Any chance you know someone who might be interested and available to help?"

A smile crept to his lips. "It just so happens I know a guy. Perfect for the job. He'll be thrilled to help."

"Glad to hear," she said, pleasure rushing through her. "Now, before I ask my second question,

I want you to know that I will understand if the answer is no. All of us have our own lives and our own journeys. Sometimes our journeys line up and sometimes they don't. Please know that I recognize and accept that, completely and fully."

She could tell he wanted to speak — almost like he knew what she was about to ask and wanted to shout out the answer. But instead, with difficulty, he managed to restrain himself — barely.

"So here's my question," she said, her heart pounding. *Why was this so hard?* Finally, she said:

"Would you like to go on a date with me?"

His eyes lit up. "A date. Like, a real date?"

She held his gaze, hope surging. "Yes, a real date."

"Yes," he said. "Yes yes *yes*." Then, as if unable to hold back for even a second longer, he wrapped his arms around her and pulled her in close. "I would love to go on a date with you, Abby Donovan."

"I'm so glad," she whispered as she welcomed his embrace, his strength feeling so good.

"There's something I'd like to say as well," he said, his hands still on her waist, pulling back to look her full in the face.

Her heart thumped. "Please, go ahead."

"From the moment we met," he said, his voice quiet yet full of emotion, "and I mean from the first moment, right there in your chocolate shop, I felt a connection with you. It wasn't something I ever expected to feel again. It took me by surprise." He swallowed, collecting himself. "As we got to know each other, I learned what a wonderful woman you are — smart, compassionate, determined, beautiful. I saw how much you care about your friends and how much your friends care about you. And when I saw how the kids responded to you, I knew I couldn't let this chance pass us by."

Tears threatened as she absorbed his words. "I'm so glad to hear you say that."

"Last night, after we got home from the chocolate lesson, the Buckley family sat down for a heart-to-heart talk."

"You did?" she said, her breath catching.

"The kids called the meeting, not me," he said, his eyes shining with emotion. "They sat me down and told me they want me to start dating again."

Stunned, she whispered, "They said that?"

"They said they wanted me to be happy again. They said their mom will always be in their hearts — they'll love and honor and cherish her always. They told me they're ready for us to move forward as a family and embrace all that life can offer." He shook his head and let out a short laugh. "My kids said that — to me. Can you believe that? I have such amazing kids."

"You do," she said, tearing up.

"And here's the kicker. They had a suggestion. More like a strong recommendation."

Abby went still. "They did?"

"They told me — ordered me, really — to ask a certain person out on a date when I saw her tonight."

Her heart was racing now. "And?"

"I was about to do just that when she walked in here a minute ago and beat me to the punch."

Abby laughed out loud, joy rushing through her.

"Now, about this date we're gonna go on," he said, his arms tightening around her. "I'm not up on the latest dating etiquette, but the way I hear it, there's supposed to be an order to things."

"An order to things?"

His expression became intent. "First we meet for coffee, then for dinner. At some point there's a hug goodnight, and then maybe…."

She flushed as she realized where he was going.

"We haven't had our first date yet," he said, leaning in, his voice low. "But there's something I really want to do — right now. Something *not* in keeping with the order of things."

"What's that?" she whispered.

"I want to do — *this*." Then he closed in for —

Their first kiss. As his lips claimed hers, she wrapped her arms around his neck and pulled him in closer, reveling in how good his embrace felt, his strength so solid and reassuring. Had she ever felt so safe, so wanted, so needed?

His lips left hers and he whispered, "Merry Christmas, Abby."

"Merry Christmas, John." Then his lips found hers again and she knew, with every ounce of her heart and soul, that together they would find their way to their dream future filled with love and belonging.

And then, from the foot of the stairs, she heard an excited gasp and a little girl whispering, "Jacob, come here! They're kissing! He did it!"

THE END

MURDER SO DEEP

EAGLE COVE MYSTERIES #1

Why is there a body in the basement?!?

When a home renovation project unearths a
mummified corpse, Sarah Boone has no choice but
to dig in deeper to find the culprit.

Get it now at Amazon!

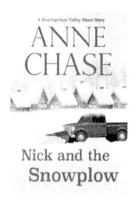

A Heartsprings Valley Short Story

ANNE
CHASE

Nick and the
Snowplow

A heartwarming holiday story about a handsome veterinarian and the shy, beautiful librarian he meets on Christmas Eve....

Nick and the Snowplow is a companion to *Christmas to the Rescue!*, the first novel in the Heartsprings Valley Winter Tale series. In *Christmas to the Rescue!*, a young librarian named Becca gets caught in a blizzard on Christmas Eve, finds shelter with a handsome veterinarian named Nick, and ends up experiencing the most surprising, adventure-filled night of her life.

Nick and the Snowplow, told from Nick's point of view, shows what happens after Nick brings Becca home at the end of their whirlwind evening.

This story is available FOR FREE when you sign up for Anne Chase's email newsletter.

Go to AnneChase.com to sign up and get your free story.

ABOUT THE AUTHOR

Greetings! I grew up in a small town (pop: 2,000) and now live in the bustling Bay Area. I write romances and mysteries, including:

The *Heartsprings Valley* romances: Celebrating love at Christmas in a small New England town.

The *Eagle Cove Mysteries:* An inquisitive cafe owner gets dragged into in murder and mayhem.

The *Emily Livingston Mysteries:* Intrigue and danger amidst the glamour and beauty of Europe.

My email newsletter is a great way to find out about upcoming books. Go to **AnneChase.com** to sign up.

Thank you for being a reader!

Printed in Great Britain
by Amazon